BUBBLES OF TERROR

Cavanaugh was already having a difficult time trying to keep the *Triton* operating properly. Haller glanced at the screen again. "Ram them if you can," he ordered.

Cavanaugh set the screen in front of him, and brought the ship around. Ahead lay a group of the bubble men on their boards. He lined them up and began heading for them, driving the ship at full speed.

The move must have been unexpected. The sea men looked back just as the *Triton* came bearing down. Don saw one open his mouth in surprise. Then the *Triton* hit.

The men in the bubbles were tossed aside instantly, while the *Triton* ploughed through the space where they had been. Don felt sick, but he switched to a rear pickup. He brought his eyes back to the screen reluctantly—and let out a surprised cry.

The bubble men had not been hurt! They had taken the full impact of the *Triton* without a sign of strain. Now they were reforming, and one of them was grinning savagely at the ship . . .

Also by Lester del Rey
Published by Ballantine Books:

Attack from Atlantis

Lester del Rey

A Del Rey Book

BALLANTINE BOOKS ● NEW YORK

A Del Rey Book
Published by Ballantine Books

Library of Congress Catalog Card Number: 53-9312

ISBN: 0-345-27448-2

This edition published by arrangement with Holt, Rinehart and Winston, Inc.

Manufactured in the United States of America

First Ballantine Books Edition: June 1978

Cover art by Dean Ellis

To
George and Doña

CONTENTS

CHAPTER 1 /

Test Run

SOMEWHERE south of Puerto Rico in the Caribbean, everything looked like a peaceful scene painted on canvas. In the background was an island covered with a surprising number of what seemed to be fishermen's houses and some kind of sheds. On the surface of the calm blue ocean, a small ship cruised along slowly, its motor throttled down until the drone of a plane far above could be heard. Except for that, the ocean seemed deserted.

The plane was up there to see that it stayed deserted. The strong-jawed young man bending over the radar screen never looked up. Another man stayed poised over a radio set, busily in contact with someone, but ready to warn off any chance craft that wandered into this particular section of the ocean.

Aboard the converted naval power boat, Don Miller was almost surrounded by radio, radar and sonar equipment. The hot sun had been pouring through the decks, and even the fan had proved of little help. He was stripped to the waist and sweating profusely, but he was still grinning as he finished a routine report to the plane and switched over to another receiver.

"First test finished," the speaker announced. "We'll surface in about fifteen minutes. All clear up there?"

"All clear," Don reported. He switched off and

reached for a towel, without taking his eyes off the sonar screen. Sound waves were emitted from equipment below the water line, and their echoes were picked up and interpreted on the screen to show the presence of any foreign object in the water. Except for one large spot, all seemed clear. The spot indicated the source of the communication he had just finished.

Don was hard-muscled and tanned to a deep brown from his belt to his black, crew-cut hair. He was a trifle shorter than average, though the supple leanness of his body made him seem taller. Track at college and swimming for hours every day during his stay here had left him in tiptop condition. It showed in his steady nerves, as he handled the equipment before him, and in the clearness of his dark gray eyes. He patted the sonar screen fondly and grinned. At seventeen, it was good to have a chance to put his knowledge to good use, without anyone standing over him, telling him what to do.

A dog lay at his feet, panting in the heat. Shep was as black as Don't hair, and his schipperke ancestry showed in a general air of cocky self-assurance; he looked like a small, jaunty Belgian shepherd. But now he lifted his head and growled faintly.

Don swung his head around, to see a round-faced, heavy man in immaculate white naval uniform emerging from the fore cabin. He was smiling doubtfully. Behind the officer, Dr. Simpson moved into view, motioning toward Don. "My nephew, Don Miller," he said to the other, and then smiled at Don. "Don, this is Admiral Haller."

Don had seen Haller come aboard, but he'd been too busy communicating with the ship that brought the officer to have time then for introductions. Now Haller's handshake was firm and friendly, but his eyes were weighing the younger man. "Glad to know you, Don. I'm sorry I had to arrive here in the middle of things, with no chance to meet everyone before. I thought at first you were a little young for all this, but you seem to be doing a good job."

"I'm almost eighteen," Don began. Then he saw his

uncle's grin and realized how foolish that must sound to the admiral. An admiral? Suddenly he realized how important this test must be, if it rated so high an officer for official observer.

"Don knows his stuff," his uncle said quickly. "He's been getting ready for our first real run for three years. He's been licensed for everything since he was sixteen. Now he's taking some advanced courses in communications physics and keeping up with young men a lot older than he is."

Don's uncle was also stripped to the waist. He was nearly bald, and he wore a small gray mustache. But in spite of that and his age of nearly fifty, he looked surprisingly like Don. He had been both father and mother to the boy since Don's parents were killed years before in an auto accident. To the world, he was a leading naval engineer and a metallurgical physicist; but Don was happy thinking of him as just Uncle Eddy.

The speaker came to life suddenly, snapping the boy back to his job. The message was coming in from the big set, which was equipped with an elaborate scrambling affair to make the message unintelligible to anyone without such equipment. "Surfacing," it announced.

Don acknowledged. His uncle and Admiral Haller were already at the rail of the boat. He set the equipment to buzz for him if a signal came in and ran quickly to a spot where he could see the ocean beside them.

At first, there was only the tiny buoy that carried the antenna for the submarine below, connected by a thin, insulated wire. Its nearness showed that the submarine would surface beside them.

Then a vague shadow appeared in the water ahead and began to take on sharper outlines as the sub rose upward at a steep angle. The buoy jerked as the wire was reeled in. The periscope broke the surface and began sliding down, until it fitted flush with the deck as the undersea boat leveled off and floated on the surface.

It was less than a hundred and fifty feet long, and seemed to be nothing but a slim, gray platform of metal, rising a foot from the surface—something like a huge torpedo. Then the conning turret, containing the bridge and periscope, was raised to a height of about ten feet above the deck, and it looked a little more like the usual picture of a submarine.

A hatch over the bridge opened, and the sharp-featured, blond head of Oliver Drake came into view. The designer of the ship's unusual atomic power plant waved at them. "How are we doing from your end? Everything's smooth as silk here."

"Doing fine, Ollie," Dr. Simpson called back. "No trouble?"

"Not a bit—except Hawkes started seeing men in bubbles outside—at four hundred fathoms! Do you think I should take her down further?"

Simpson nodded. "It's up to you. And tell Hawkes—"

But the hatch had snapped shut already. The conning tower was retracted and the submarine began diving, briefly showing the name on her stern—*Triton I*. Then she was gone, with the little antenna buoy streaking out behind her.

Don ducked back to his radio equipment to keep in touch. He heard his uncle and Admiral Haller move by as he was making checks.

"So that's it," the admiral was saying, and his voice was disappointed. "What's so special? I didn't have much chance to study the papers they gave me after Baylor had his accident and I got rushed in to replace him. Suppose you brief me."

They moved on, out of Don's earshot, but he could imagine his uncle's answer.

The *Triton* was hardly a novelty in being an atomic-powered submarine; the *Nautilus* had been first, and that was many years ago now. But all the previous atomic subs had simply used an atomic pile to heat steam for their turbines, replacing the older diesel engines and electric motors; the engines had been no more than power sources to drive a propeller that moved the vessel through the water. And there, the *Triton* differed.

Drake had invented the system. On the little *Triton*, a very small and special atomic pile of his design was operating at the highest temperature ever used, generating heat from broken atoms. The heat was used to turn the water into steam—but that steam was then used as a jet, blasting back through special nozzles at the rear and forcing the *Triton* ahead exactly as a jet engine moved a plane.

Furthermore, the water so heated was drawn directly out of the ocean. Developing ways to handle that sea water and let it become steam without leaving its salts as blocking deposits had required the combined ability of Drake and Don's uncle.

The result had been to eliminate all the complicated turbines and motors—leaving only a small generator to provide electricity for light and controls. It also made the ship far more nearly automatic than anything that had gone before. The *Triton* could probably cruise twenty times around the world without surfacing, or without anyone needing to go near the heavily shielded power plant.

Dr. Simpson had designed the hull, using new alloys of metal and new methods of adding strength, to create a ship that could go to great depths without requiring enormously heavy construction. The two men had met some ten years ago, and each had found the other's ideas dovetailing perfectly with his own. Now, finally, the result of their labors was being tested.

"Four hundred fathoms," the speaker announced. That meant they were twenty-four hundred feet below the surface.

Haller and Simpson had come up now and were listening in carefully. The speaker began giving a series of figures on pressure, the strain indicated by hull gauges, and everything else that had to be known.

"Speed thirty knots, depth five hundred," Drake's voice said. "This is it, Ed—three thousand feet, and we're running thirteen hundred pounds pressure on every square inch. Not a groan out of her. Thrity-five hundred feet now . . ."

"Better bring her back up," Simpson said into the microphone, leaning over Don's shoulder. "That's enough for first test. We'll have to go over her inch by inch to see how she takes it before going further."

"Right, Ed. Up we come. We—*Hey, come about! Over there!*"

There were sounds of confusion suddenly, and Drake's voice was shouting from some distance beyond his microphone. Don felt the hairs on his neck lift as he imagined a leak at that pressure. With fifteen hundred pounds per square inch—a hundred times normal atmospheric pressure—a pinhole would let in a stream that could cut through sheet steel. "Calling *Triton,*" he said tensely into the mike. *"Triton!"*

Drake's voice was back almost at once. "Sorry. I thought I saw something. It looked like—well, it looked like a man inside a bubble out there! The same thing Hawkes thought he saw. No trace now. Must be some odd fish that lives down here."

"Probably," Simpson agreed. He had picked up Don's towel and was mopping the sudden flood of perspiration off his face, but he kept his voice calm. "Bring her up, Ollie."

"Right." There was the sound of a switch. Then the speaker went dead.

Haller shook his head. "Maybe the feeling of being down there in all that pressure is getting to them," he suggested. "They aren't trained for it, like regular submariners."

"They shouldn't both have seen the same thing, if it's just imagination," Simpson said doubtfully. "Or maybe Hawkes' words did suggest it to Ollie. No, it's probably just what Ollie said—some kind of fish we haven't found yet. What's the sonar indicate, Don?"

Don had been trying to discover that himself. "It doesn't say," he admitted, with a touch of worry. "There's a cold and warm current mixing somewhere between us, and it's making a cold wall that deflects the sonar beam. Uncle Eddy, suppose there are men who can get down there?"

Simpson chuckled, though his eyes showed traces of uncertainty. "Suppose Shep can suddenly fly, Don! Not at those depths. A hundred fathoms is about the limit. That pressure would . . ."

The speaker interrupted him. "Ed!" Drake's voice barked tautly. "Ed, the *Triton* won't answer her controls. Something's wrong with the stern diving plane, and the bow plane has snapped its cable. Wait a minute, I'm getting an observation on it now . . . Stuck! There's something that looks like a metal rod stuck in the bow plane somehow."

"Is she equipped with normal trim tanks?" Haller asked quickly. At Simpson's nod, he swung about to face Don. "Tell him to blow out his bow tanks and come up under power."

Shep growled faintly again at the roughness of the admiral's voice. Don touched him reassuringly and began relaying the orders.

Haller was muttering something about civilians in command of a ship, but he kept most of his unhappiness to himself. Don started to resent it; then he realized Haller hadn't gotten to be an admiral in the submarine service without knowing his business. With the bow lightened, the *Triton* should tilt to climb.

"Trying that," Drake's answer came. "The tank valve is stuck, too."

"Then flood the stern tanks," Haller ordered. He turned to face Simpson again. "I take it you have power enough to make up for any extra weight."

"Plenty of power," Simpson answered.

Don's hands were sweating as he relayed instructions, and he snapped a quick look to see that his uncle was frowning tensely. But Haller seemed unworried. "Will they be all right, sir?" he asked.

"Plenty of things left to do," Haller told him. "They can always blow out the main ballast tanks enough to lighten the ship and float her. But it's better to come up under power. Ah!"

An indication had come onto the sonar screen. Don saw that the *Triton* was no longer masked by the cold wall. He switched on his microphone. "Report!"

"Coming up," Drake said. "But she's a little sluggish

with the stern tanks flooded. She's—*Hey!*" He was quiet for a second, then resumed. "Two of those fish, or whatever they are. Just caught a glimpse of them in the rear screen. They still look like men in bubbles. Gone now, though—must be fast. Ah, the stern plane is working again. That's better. Depth two thousand, and coming up steadily now. Ed, I'm going to head straight back to the dock as soon as I reach five hundred feet. I'm pulling in the antenna, so there'll be no surface trace. See you there."

He cut off, but the sonar showed that he was still coming up, now under complete control, and heading toward the dock on the island. Haller watched the screen for a few moments, nodded, and went back toward the rear of the boat. Simpson accepted a cup of coffee from one of the men and dropped onto a seat near his nephew.

"Are we still going to run the official test?" Don asked. This was only a preliminary test run to show up any faults before the full test was made with observers on board the *Triton*. The ship now had only the barest skeleton crew of five aboard. Don had wanted to go on this trial run, but had reluctantly agreed to wait, since he was needed here.

Simpson nodded. "Probably. We'll go over her tonight and tomorrow to see if we can figure what happened. But unless the bugs are worse than it seems, we should be able to run the full-dress test day after tomorrow."

They were heading back to the island now, with the sonar screen showing the *Triton* cruising along below the surface toward the dock there. Under the camouflage of simple fishermen's huts and sheds, the little island had been turned into a small but efficient shipyard for assembling the submarine and tending her.

Actually, most of the camouflage was fairly recent. When Drake and Simpson began working, nobody had felt any need for secrecy, and the huts and sheds had been temporary things; they'd been put up simply because such buildings made for both comfort and economy in this climate. And the island had been chosen because it belonged to the company that was funding the preliminary work.

Things had changed when the Navy got interested and began backing the research. By then, it was too late to keep the project completely secret, but they had managed to make it seem that little progress was being made. Now, if the presence of an admiral here meant what Don suspected, the Navy was about to take over completely, and that would mark the end of the freedom the men here had once shared. Security would probably refuse to let him near the future research that might be done. It was probably a good thing for Drake and his uncle, since they'd now be able to command anything they needed. But he couldn't really look forward to it.

Apparently Simpson had also been nursing unhappy thoughts. He sighed now and stood up slowly.

"Don," he said reluctantly, "I'm afraid I've got bad news for you. I've been talking to Haller, and we're going to have more observers than I expected. And the Navy wants to put on its own crew, too—men who've had a lot of experience in the submarine service. I suppose that makes sense, but . . ."

"You mean I can't go along?" Don asked slowly. At his uncle's faint nod, he bent further over his screens, hiding his face.

He'd worked like a fool for three years to qualify, and the *Triton* had been the biggest thing in his life for long before that. But he knew his uncle couldn't help the way things had now turned out—probably nobody could—and he tried to sound casual as he managed to shrug. "Okay, then, I don't go."

Simpson's hand dropped onto his shoulder. "I'm sorry, Don. Everything will be made up somehow."

Don nodded, but he knew better. Nothing could ever make up for his not being on either of the test runs. If he could even have seen those things that looked like men in bubbles . . .

Then he got suddenly busy as the boat approached the island.

CHAPTER 2 /

Operation Depth

DURING THE TEN YEARS since Don had first seen the island, it had been constantly changing. Originally, when Simpson and Drake first won their grant to begin research on the submarine, it had been occupied mostly by fishermen, and the company that owned it had done little with it. But the little cove that broke the shoreline was surprisingly deep, making an ideal place for the work on the ship. The dock had been rebuilt and enlarged, and construction men had replaced the fishers. Then most of them had gone, to be replaced in turn by the men and engineers needed for early work. Lately that work force had expanded as more and more men arrived to help with the assembling of the ship from the parts that were shipped out from factories back on the mainland.

Now that work was finished, and most of the latest crew was gone. It was a different place. Don had made friends through the years on his visits here from school, with new ones replacing those who left. But now almost all the faces seemed strange. All the hard hats had been replaced by uniform caps with official insigne, it seemed. The bustle and activity went on, but it was official now, and Don seemed left out of things.

He wandered about, feeling lost in the shuffle. He'd

11

never before known what it was like to be on the outside looking in.

There was a feeling in the air that worried him, also. He'd read about it, but had never experienced it before. The cold war and the little hot wars had all ended before he could remember, and the world had relaxed for a time. Even the security checks of those grimmer days had slowly been relaxed. There had been none of the dim, dark feeling of war—until lately. The *Triton* had been planned for peaceful exploration of the sea; and even the Navy's initial interest had not been centered on her value as a potential weapon.

Lately, though, tension had been growing again, and all controls were tightening up. Don had been only vaguely aware of that, since the *Triton* had taken up so much of his thought and time. But he was beginning to realize that if he hadn't already been on the island, mixed up in the building of the ship, he probably would have been forbidden to go there. Everything connected with atomic power or capable of being turned into a weapon was going quickly under official security wraps, due to the worsening condition of relations with other nations that had never been properly explained.

"Hi, Miller!" a voice called, breaking into his unpleasant reflections. He turned to see the long, lanky figure of Sid Upjohn, the only reporter to be admitted for the official test. Upjohn usually looked lazy and careless, but there was a keen brain under his wild thatch of red hair. He'd been the leading science writer for a chain of newspapers for the last eight years, and even the scientists respected him for his understanding and honesty. He had visited the island a couple of times before, and he knew most of the old crowd who still remained.

"All the bugs straightened out?" the reporter asked.

Don nodded. "Looks like it. You probably know better than I do." The ship had apparently stood the first test beautifully, except for the exhaust valve that had temporarily failed on the bow trim tank. As for the diving planes . . .

Nobody had figured that out, so far as Don knew. Both stern and bow planes showed signs of having had something jammed into their hinges, and there were bits of copper left in the marks. But copper didn't float around in the sea to be rammed against by accident. He remembered Drake's report on the metal bar that had been reported in the bow planes.

It almost looked like sabotage. Yet, unless it could be admitted that the "men in bubbles" had been real men, the whole idea was ridiculous. Haller's idea that the ship must have run into a bit of old wreckage seemed equally ridiculous, though perhaps easier to believe; but the ship hadn't been near the bottom where wrecks might be found. At any event, such matters weren't ones Don could discuss with the reporter.

"They don't intend to go so far down this time, so the trip should be safe enough," he told Upjohn. "You'll be going out tomorrow all right."

"Yeah. I'm sorry you won't be coming with us, Don. Met your replacement yet?" As Don shook his head, Upjohn jerked his thumb back toward the mess hall. "Then come on, I'll introduce him. I've met everyone by now who's going. I was telling him about you, by the way."

They went inside and dropped down at a table where a young man in a Navy uniform was drinking a cup of black coffee. "Don Miller, this is Jim Ricks," Upjohn introduced them. "How do you feel now, Jim?"

The man grinned. "Lousy," he answered. "Hi, Don. Remember me?"

Don frowned as he studied the other. Then slowly recognition came. Ricks had been a senior on the high-school track team when Don had first gone out as a freshman. "Glad you're replacing me," he said, trying to sound sincere.

"I'm not. I feel like a first-class heel, taking something you earned," Ricks said. "If I could, I'd pull out fast."

The talk then switched by mutual consent, to earlier times when they were at school. When Don finally got up to return to his uncle's house, Upjohn joined him. They moved along in silence, until Shep's barking caught Don's ears. He hurried around a corner of the street and to his house.

But the dog was only enjoying himself, barking in pleasure. Admiral Haller, still in spotless clothes, was squatting down and throwing a stick for the dog to fetch. Shep's normal hostility to strangers had completely disappeared. He broke off to greet Don happily, and then went back to the game with the stick.

"Hello, Don—Upjohn," Haller said casually, standing up and brushing dust from his hands. "Hope you don't mind my having a bit of fun with your dog? I had a schipperke when I was growing up and I'm rather partial to them."

"He seems to like you." Don's liking for the man had increased considerably. Usually Shep was reserved around strangers.

Upjohn motioned back toward the visitors' building. "I see the last of the observers has arrived, Admiral. I'm glad to see that the President sent Dexter to represent him—I've worked with him before, and he's a good man. How come they sent Senator Kenney, though? I thought Meredith was supposed to be scheduled for this junket. He's the one who should represent his committee. Why Kenney?"

Don had met the two men briefly earlier that morning, and his own impression fitted Upjohn's reaction. Dexter, the science advisor to the President, had seemed like a successful businessman of the nicer sort; but Senator Kenney acted as if all the world was peopled by fools who were in some kind of conspiracy against him.

"I don't know any more about it than you do," Haller answered. "I had nothing to do with the selection; I don't rate high enough for that. In fact, I have very little choice in saying who can go and who can't." He smiled at Don, half-apologetically, and then was serious again. "Don, everyone who knows anything about the ship except you is busy getting the *Triton* ready. I was wondering if you'd be good enough to show me around the ship before the test. Upjohn, if you'd like to come with us . . ."

"I suppose a little guided tour wouldn't hurt. Might help me to learn what I'm not supposed to report," Upjohn agreed. "And that seems to be the important thing nowadays—knowing enough not to give away too much. Fine life for a reporter."

They headed for the *Triton,* where men were going over every inch of her in the concealed dock. Shep bounded along behind, sniffing happily as they entered the ship. He was familiar with it, but there were always new things to smell, it seemed. He trotted ahead and was soon lost to sight.

Don spent most of the day showing the two men over the craft. It was smaller and simpler than most submarines, but there was still a lot to be seen. At the last possible opportunity, she'd been redesigned to handle torpedoes, and the tubes filled the nose, with the torpedo room behind that. It was another unwelcome sign of the mounting tension in the world.

Then came quarters for the crew. Just in front of the conning turret was the captain's room, an officers' wardroom and the little galley where all food was prepared. Below lay the crew's mess hall, and at the bottom were storage rooms for immense amounts of food and other necessities. The conning turret was the bridge, navigating room, control room, radar-sonar room, with the periscope housing taking up much of the center. Behind the turret lay other bunkrooms and the small engine-control room. The rear of the ship was devoted to the atomic power unit, sealed off by thick layers of shielding—though less than had been necessary with previous atomic piles.

There was one other new idea, however. Under the conning turret and the stores, a low space had been left. This was filled with layers of shallow tanks in which lush green plants were growing under banks of lighting. Men had been talking about using such plants to maintain breathable air for many years, but this would be the first test of the system. The plants had been developed by geneticists and other scientists working for the space agencies, but no space ship had yet made use of them. The idea was obvious, of course—men used up oxygen and gave off carbon dioxide, while the plants reversed this, keeping the air fresh and breathable. With this and the atomic drive, the ship could theoretically stay under the surface for years at a time.

But like all submarines, the *Triton* was a complicated machine. There were trim tanks and ballast tanks where the amount of water admitted could regulate the way the ship floated, sank or leveled off. There were pipes and fittings everywhere, control valves, small motors, escape hatches, a garbage ejector, windlasses, machinery to drive the diving planes—things that looked like the wing controls on airplanes but were much heavier—and a host of other things to fill the space. No spot seemed completely free. And nothing could ever be large enough, though the *Triton* was more comfortable than some subs. The absence of complicated engine equipment and oxygen supplies had helped, at least.

It was late when they finally left the ship, but Don had the feeling that Haller had already mastered her. The admiral held out a hand as they parted. "Thanks, Don. You were a splendid guide. I wish you were coming along."

"He should be," Upjohn commented.

"So almost everyone has been telling me," Haller said. "Don, I'd change the schedule, if I could. But except in matters of emergency, I have to stick to the assignments made for me. Ricks is listed for the job, and I have to use him."

Don understood, and felt no anger at Haller. He wished they'd all drop the subject. He'd been trying not to think about it, though he hadn't succeeded very well. He went up to his room and tried to work up some interest in a new signal shifter for his radio equipment, but he couldn't concentrate on the diagram. He'd always enjoyed electronics, but his real drive had been spent in trying to get ready to be part of the crew on the first official test of the *Triton*. Now it all seemed pointless.

He finally gave up and went to bed, not even bothering to go down to eat. Shep curled up beside the bed where Don's fingers could reach his neck. He seemed to sense his master's feelings, since he licked at Don's hand.

But in the morning, Don forced himself to look cheerful as he stood watching the final preparations. Haller was busy inspecting things, with Drake and Simpson beside him. Most of the men going aboard were ones in uniform whom Don had barely met. The cook, two crewmen, Kayne, the navigator, and the black helmsman, Cavanaugh. Only Drake, Simpson and the master mechanic, Walrich, were men who had helped build the *Triton*.

Ricks came up late, nodding to Don. He went immediately to Haller, and there was a brief conversation. Then he turned away and Haller motioned for Don to come forward.

"An emergency has come up," he said. His face remained grave, though there seemed to be a smile barely suppressed. "My electronics man seems to have a touch of food poisoning. Apparently he is not in condition to perform his duties properly. Unfortunately, we have no official replacement. Mr. Miller, I wonder if you might be willing to volunteer?"

Don gulped, and felt his knees turn to jelly under him. He should have guessed, perhaps; Upjohn's earlier wink and his uncle's smiles had obviously been hints. But it came as a complete surprise. He swallowed twice before he could answer, and he could feel a foolish smile of pleasure creep onto his face. "I—I'd be happy to volunteer, sir!"

"Good. Then get anything you need and report back on board in ten minutes, Mr. Miller." This time Haller smiled back at him. Upjohn and his uncle were also smiling. Only the thin, bilious face of Senator Kenney remained unhappy. Kenney was looking on with displeasure at the interruption to bringing his luggage aboard.

Simpson caught his nephew's arm and drew him aside. "By a strange coincidence, I happened to find a bag of your stuff already packed and down here, Don," he said. "Upjohn told me Ricks and he had plans last night, and I thought Haller might go along with them. But don't let on that it was a put-up job!"

Don located Ricks as the other was about to leave and tried to thank him. But Ricks was playing it very straight, acting as if he really were sick. "Got to report to sick bay," he said. "I'm glad you were here to replace me. Have a four-oh test, Don!"

Don found himself assigned to the bunk he'd originally been scheduled for. He put the bag his uncle had packed into his locker, wondering why he'd need so much for a simple test run. Then he remembered that there'd been talk of sealed orders, involving a trial of several days duration. He doubted this, but it was probably smart to be prepared for anything.

He reported to Haller in the captain's stateroom—if the little room deserved such a name—and was given the routine assignment to the sonar-radar section. It was partitioned off with a door to insure some quiet for study of the signals. He dropped to his seat and stared about him. He'd been there a thousand times, but it all looked new now. The hum of the air-conditioning machinery blended with other muffled sounds of a ship getting ready to move. And the smell of metal, oil and machinery had a new meaning.

Mr. Miller, electronics officer of the *Triton*, all set for Operation Depth!

He heard the closing of the after hatch and watched the hands of the chronometer creep around to the hour of ten. Three minutes more and they'd be on their way.

Then there was a sudden yell that blended with the closing of the fore hatch. The annunciator in the radar room announced: "All hatches closed. Lower the turret!"

But Don was on his feet before the big conning turret began sliding down to fit flush with the deck. From the bow of the *Triton* had come the shouts of men mixed with the barking of a dog!

Almost at once, there was a scratching on the door of the room. He threw it open, and Shep came bounding in, leaping up to lick his hand. The annunciator spoke again, but he didn't hear it. He felt the shudder of the ship, but it barely registered.

Beyond the dog stood one of the new crewmen and Senator Kenney. And Kenney was fuming in outrage at the idea of a dog sneaking aboard at the last moment. "Get him off, at once!" he ordered the crewman.

A metal door opened then, and Admiral Haller came through it. "What's going on here?" he demanded. Then his eyes fastened on the bouncing form of the dog, and leaped up to meet Don's. "Oh," he said, "a stowaway!"

Don picked up the dog. He might have known that it was too good to last. They'd probably decide he was a hopeless child, more interested in bringing his pet aboard than doing his duty. And then he'd be sent ashore with Shep, while Ricks was hastily summoned back.

"I'm sorry, sir," he said weakly and started through the door.

CHAPTER 3 /

Trouble on the Triton

HALLER stopped him before he could leave. "Were you responsible for this, Mr. Miller?"

"I didn't bring Shep on board, sir," Don answered, and something in the tone Haller had used made him more hopeful. "He just slipped in, I guess. I'm sorry——"

"See that he keeps out of the way," the admiral ordered. He was interrupted by a stream of protests from Kenney, but shrugged them aside. "We're under way, on official orders, and I don't intend to put about. Anyhow, I don't see how it can cause trouble, and Upjohn will have something to write about. If you'll return to your quarters until we reach depth, Senator . . ."

Kenney spun around and stalked off, muttering something about future appropriations. Don had to agree with Upjohn. Most Senators were good men, as he knew from a group who had visited the island two years before. It was a shame that Kenney had to be the one to go along.

Haller grinned faintly at Don, and turned back to control. "Take her down," his words drifted back. Don shut the door of the radar room and returned to his work, with Shep lying quietly at his feet. The sonar screen showed that they were already well away from the island. He flipped on the television viewing panel—the *Triton* ran under the surface without ports, but with a number of television pickups that could be tuned in on the viewing panels. They were already diving, and there was nothing but water around them.

The *Triton* could move downward in a hurry when set for it; now she must have had both stern and bow planes set for descent, and was heading down in a leisurely way on even keel. The water grew darker as they dropped, and he had to set the gain up on the viewing panel. At daybreak, there had been the threat of a storm, and it must have been brewing up above, since it was growing darker than it should have been. At two hundred fathoms, the outside lights were cut on ahead of them.

This time, they were not trying to maintain radio contact with the surface. The antenna was stowed away with its miles of thin, insulated wire—insulated with a plastic which held enough air to make it weigh the same as the water it displaced, so there would be no strain on it. It would be used only for emergencies now.

Haller's voice suddenly came over the annunciator. "We're on open orders now, gentlemen. We'll cruise in the neighborhood of the Milwaukee Deep, and take echo-soundings to maintain an accurate chart of our course. We will simulate certain maneuvers and return to port in forty-eight hours."

The Milwaukee Deep lay north of Puerto Rico, reaching a depth of five and a half miles in some places. Don wondered what would happen if a submarine got out of control there and sank all the way. But he knew the answer—even the *Triton* couldn't stand a pressure of thirteen thousand pounds per square inch; she'd be squashed flat before she reached bottom. Probably the area had been chosen as the least likely spot for the test of a new submarine—and hence the best place for secrecy.

They were down to four hundred fathoms now, nearly half a mile. Now and then, fish could be seen in the lights of the ship—strange fish, unlike those found at the surface or shallower waters. Don kept glancing at them, but they were somewhat familiar from numerous pictures that had been taken by remote control and from bathyspheres—the heavy, round, hollow steel balls barely big enough to hold a man which had gone down to greater depths than the *Triton* had yet reached, though not as comfortably.

Down here, the water stayed at a uniform temperature of 39° Fahrenheit, no matter what the surface conditions. No sunlight could reach such depths in any amount that could support plant life. The plankton that supported most of the upper life drifted down from above, however, along with bits of other life. Down here, plants and animals were scavengers.

Don kept careful track of their progress, reporting the information from the sonar screen and the echo-sound device regularly. But his interest still centered on the viewing panel. He was looking for the "man in the bubble." It was still a mystery to them all, particularly since the unexplained metal traces had turned up on the diving planes.

At five hundred fathoms, they leveled off and proceeded along an even course, ticking off a steady thirty knots an hour. Don began working with his listening devices, trying to determine how much noise was produced by the *Triton*. It seemed nearly undetectable. He released a listening device from a rear compartment and let it trail them for fifteen minutes before having it rewind. The jets of steam and water that drove the *Triton* were so well designed that they were practically noiseless, and the ship itself slipped through the water with no projections to cause trouble. The *Triton* would be almost undetectable, fortunately.

Normal practice called for four hours of watch, with eight hours off. But the *Triton* was only a test ship, and had been designed originally for oceanographic surveys, rather than as a weapon. Most of her machinery was so automatic that a minimum crew of twelve was enough; on this run, observers had swelled the ranks, and made less room available for the crew. There were only ten aboard who could do the work that had to be done. Officers and crew would have to work most of the time on this run, catching barely time for sleep.

Upjohn came slouching in a couple of hours later. Haller had issued orders that he was to have complete freedom of the ship, so Don let him in.

"Go stretch your legs, kid," the reporter suggested. "I asked the skipper, and he says I can take over here for a while. I used to be able to handle this stuff well enough. Anyhow, nothing much will be done until we fix the depth controls."

Don got up, glad to move around. But he frowned. "What's wrong?"

"I gather they've found that they can't blow their trim tanks again, and they're trying to find out why. No trouble now, but it could be, later. So we're idling along. Go on and see for yourself."

"No men in bubbles?" Don asked, grinning.

Upjohn stared at him thoughtfully. Then he shrugged. "As a matter of fact, I thought I saw one in the bow viewing panel just before they found the trouble. But it could have been anything, I guess. Heck, we were bound to have trouble. I figured out there are just thirteen of us aboard!"

"You don't believe that superstition, do you?" Don asked, but he was pretty sure of the answer.

Upjohn grinned, and then sobered. "No—but if anyone on board who *is* superstitious finds out the number, we'll have accidents; that's the way it goes—men who are afraid always create the situation they're afraid of. Scram, Don, while you can. I'll call you if anything comes up."

Don hurried along the little passage toward the bow, where he heard the sounds of men at work. Walrich and his uncle were busy going over the pumps and controls for the bow trim tanks.

"Just stuck again," his uncle said in answer to Don's questions. "Apparently the valves don't work when there is enough pressure outside, though I can't figure out why. We can take on water, but we can't eject it.

Well, we'll have to change back to the older design, I guess, unless we can work the bugs out of this. Figure out how to get more torque from that motor, Walrich?"

The broad shoulders twitched slightly as the mechanic looked up. "Sure. Put in another motor and try to force the valve. I think it'll stand the extra power. But that valve should work! Well, I'll get one of the men and we'll get busy on it."

Simpson and Don went back toward the wardroom where a steaming pot of coffee stood. The older man looked worried, though there was no sign of panic. "We're already as deep as we intend to go," he said. "But I wish we were cruising higher up. I don't like the way that valve is acting. There's something funny about it. And we found some tarry stuff on it before; we put a screen over the valves this time, but it doesn't seem to help. Maybe there's something down here that we don't know about."

Drake came in and filled a cup. "There's something funny, Ed—no question about it. The main ballast tanks won't clear. Same as the trim tanks. And in testing them, we've taken on enough water to overload us already. If we stopped moving, we'd sink to the bottom right now. The diving planes are all that's holding us up."

He fished out a cigarette and stood playing with it, making no effort to light it. "Well," he said at last, "I've tried something. I suspected that tarry stuff before, and tested it. It seems to dissolve in a weak detergent solution, so I've had a few drums of the powder dumped into the tanks. Getting it in was a job, too! If it works, we're all right; there's plenty of detergent on board."

"I'd better tell Walrich to try the same, then," Simpson decided.

"Already saw him. He's working on an injector now, instead of the extra motor."

Don's uncle got up to go back, and Drake joined him. The boy started after them, and then gave up the idea. It was time he got back to the sonar controls. He picked up a sandwich and started back just as an annunciator barked out overhead. "Miller wanted in radar!"

There was a sliding panel between the main control room and the sonar room, and Don saw that it was thrown back now. Upjohn got up as he came in quickly and Don sank into the seat. Haller was watching intently from the other side of the panel.

Then he saw it on the sonar screen—a big pip that was traveling beside them, and apparently matching their course, since it stayed fixed on the screen. "Probably something wrong with the sonar," he said. It was ridiculous to think that there could be another submarine operating in these waters at this depth.

He turned to his listening devices, but there was no sound beyond the noises the fish made. Men had been surprised, at first, at the idea of fish making sounds—they were too used to thinking of sound as something that traveled only in air; but by now, every man who worked with the equipment took the fish "talk" for granted.

Then the spot on the screen moved, indicating the object was rising. It moved back again, almost at once, but it had proved that it wasn't merely a flaw in the instrument. Something was out there.

Haller issued orders to change course by ten degrees. As the *Triton* swung, the pip moved aside for a few seconds. Then it drew nearer again. It was pacing them, deliberately matching their course.

Haller picked up his microphone and put through a call for Drake, who appeared almost at once. "How's the freeing of those valves going?" he asked. Then he added, almost as an afterthought: "You don't have to answer in person, Dr. Drake, you'll save time by using the engine-room phone."

"Too early to tell about the effect of the detergent—if it can reach the tar at all. And if it *is* tar. I've put Walrich back to doubling the motors on the trim tank." Drake ran a hand through his blond hair, and grinned weakly in an effort at apology. "I forgot about the phone—wasn't in the engine room, anyhow. I'm not used to Navy methods, I guess."

"I don't expect you to be," Haller told him. "When I was sent to skipper *your* ship, I expected to throw the rule book out of the window. Anyhow, do what you can about those valves. It looks as if there's another submarine pacing us. We have to figure it's an enemy, and to expect attack!"

Drake took a look at the sonar screen and whistled. He nodded curtly and went out at a run.

"Enemy still holding position," Don reported.

Haller nodded absently. "Take her up as fast as you can—and full power," he ordered. The ship shuddered faintly as the tall helmsman threw the power lever and moved the wheel. Here, there was a direct connection from control room to power, without the need to relay orders through the engine room. The ship began climbing painfully upward, fighting against the overload of water ballast in the tanks.

"A nice ship, except for a few little bugs," Haller said quietly, as he studied Don's screens. "Too bad in a way though that the government kept its hands off so much—otherwise, we'd have her fitted for a full crew, and there'd be auxiliary standard valves until these were thoroughly tested. That's one place where Navy experience is better than private enthusiasm. We're too small a crew here for any real cruising—even for survey work. But if we get back, I'm going to recommend that we build this general type exclusively from now on. . . . Isn't it drawing closer to us now?"

"Yes, sir," Don admitted. He could feel moisture on his palms, but Haller's casualness had helped to ease some of the tension—as the admiral had probably intended. The "enemy" was definitely closer, probably not more than a quarter of a mile away.

"Aren't you going to man the torpedoes?" he asked finally.

Haller laughed grimly. "The Navy can make mistakes, too, Mr. Miller. No, there's no use manning them. We intended them only for practice tests—never expected to meet another ship at this depth—so they're not armed. No explosive charge. We don't have any weapons at all, in fact. All we can do is hope we can outrun any torpedoes they send—if they attack."

Now Don's hands really began to sweat. The pip on the screen seemed to swell up to double its size, and to be leaping out of the screen at him. He swallowed and forced his eyes to focus on it. Then he saw that it was nearer, judging by the brightness.

"It's catching up with us, sir," he reported.

"Take her down, Mr. Cavanaugh," Haller ordered. "We can't outrun them when we're fighting our weight. But maybe we can stand more pressure than they can. And keep going down until I order you to stop."

On the screen, the pip showed that the "enemy" was heading for them still, and rapidly shortening the distance. They went roaring down into the darkness of the depths, but the pip on the screen grew brighter and brighter, as whatever was behind them rapidly caught up.

CHAPTER 4/

Head-On Collision

THEY PASSED THE DEPTH of five hundred fathoms and kept going down. Don jerked his eyes from the screen and got a quick reading on the depth from the echo-sound. Here, the ocean floor lay some fifteen hundred fathoms below the surface, where the pressure would be two tons per square inch. He shivered at the idea. His uncle claimed the *Triton* should stand a depth of two miles without any danger, but he didn't want to try it yet.

The pip on the screen slipped behind them completely, then showed that the pursuer was just off the stern.

Something hit them violently. The *Triton* seemed to slew around and to tilt sharply. There was a dull rumble of sound. Don waited for the fatal noise of water hissing in, but it did not come.

"No torpedo," Haller announced. His face had tensed, but his voice was still quiet and cool. "Steady as you go, Mr. Cavanaugh." He picked up the general call microphone. "We've just been hit, but not by a torpedo. What you felt was only a deliberate collision, and we can stand a great deal of that safely, if not comfortably. In such a game, the risk is at least as great to the attacker as it is to us."

There was another heavy thump. This time, it turned

the *Triton* part way over. Don grabbed at the radar desk to keep from falling. His stomach was sick, but he held onto himself somehow.

And again the thump came. This time there were excited shouts from somewhere on the ship, but no warning gongs sounded to indicate a rupture to the seams.

Kayne, the navigator, looked up from his concentration on the dials and indicators. "Why doesn't he use torps or something?"

"Pressure, maybe," Haller answered. "We're down to seven hundred fathoms—a ton of pressure per inch. If we get far enough down, an explosive can't even explode. The pressure—"

This time the ship threatened to turn over completely. Cavanaugh and the navigator went into frantic action, but they finally came back to level.

". . . pressure outside might be greater than the explosive pressure inside the torpedo," Haller finished. "Instead of exploding, it might collapse."

"Unless he uses an atomic war head," Don muttered under his breath.

Haller heard him, however. "Unless he uses atomics," he agreed quietly.

Then there was a shout from the helmsman, and he was pointing frantically to the bow viewing plate. Don's view was blocked, but he switched his own plate rapidly over to the bow pickup.

There was no question about it. Outside, in the lights of the *Triton,* a great whale was swimming rapidly alongside and slightly ahead of them. Their "enemy" submarine was simply a huge whale.

It seemed incredible that any living thing could descend from the surface into this pressure, but he'd seen accounts that claimed the great cetaceans could descend for over a mile. The strange thing, really, was that such a large one should be in this part of the ocean. Usually they were found further north, as he remembered it.

The creature drew off to the side and suddenly came rushing at them. This time, Don switched the pickups to follow it all the way. It came charging up to the stern, striking with its great nose. Then it swung about and seemed to nuzzle against the ship.

He barely saw the last as it shook the *Triton* about, but Haller seemed to have seen the same.

"He's playing with us," the admiral said. He laughed, grimly. "Maybe he thinks we're another whale with our spouts on the wrong end! How long has he been with us?"

"About twenty minutes, sir," Don guessed.

"Good. He must be running out of air, with all the effort he's been putting out. Maybe he'll surface."

The whale wasn't surfacing yet. It turned for one last gesture of friendship to this strange invader of its home waters. But apparently it had grown tired of the stern, or the hot exhaust there had proved uncomfortable. This time its charge was straight for the bow. It met the *Triton* head on. The bow seemed to lift and twist. The whale slid under it, hitting it again with his great flukes as he passed.

That, apparently, was enough. With a sudden directness of purpose, he turned upward and began rising, until he was gone from the light of their lamps. The sonar screen showed him fading away quickly toward the surface.

But now the *Triton* had other worries. Cavanaugh was sweating and laboring at the helm, and Kayne had gotten up to assist him. The *Triton* was wobbling uncertainly, like a leaf drifting in the wind. It kept threatening to roll, and only the wild efforts on the helmsman's part were keeping it anywhere near level.

"The bow plane, sir," he gasped, nodding toward the screen. But there was only the ocean ahead showing there.

Don twisted his switch, until he found the pickup which would show the bow diving plane at the far edge. Haller bent down to study it. He gasped faintly.

"Bent," he reported. "Neutralize it and use your stern planes, Mr. Cavanaugh."

The bow plane was buckled into an odd curve, as if some giant had taken a sheet of wax and bent it in his hands. The whale must have struck it dead center.

Cavanaugh shook his head. "Can't, sir. Stern planes have been stuck since he first hit us. Been using only the bow ones."

Haller grunted as if someone had hit him in the stomach. "Cut speed. Dead slow ahead," he ordered. Some of the shaking stopped then. The trim tanks were well enough balanced to hold them level. But now they had no way to control their ascent or descent. In fact, there was no way to keep from sinking slowly downward, unless they could free the tank valves and lighten themselves.

Haller was talking with Simpson over the engine phone, but the news obviously wasn't good. He put the phone back on its cradle and swung to stare at Don's screens. Then he pulled a diagram of the *Triton's* construction from one of the little lockers and began pouring over it.

"We'll have to eject everything we can to lighten weight, and do what trimming we have to by moving things about by hand," he decided. "We'll start with the torpedoes. Better do it two at a time, with time to trim between. There's probably a storm going on up there, but we'll have to risk it."

Don felt his confidence coming back, and now he was glad that they had a man with a lot of practical experience on subs for their skipper. His uncle was a fine designer, and Drake was a wizard with atomics— but neither could have sounded as confident as Haller did; and it seemed to be a confidence that grew from the man's knowledge that there was always another answer, if the first one didn't work.

He glanced back at his screen and let out a sudden shout. Haller jerked around, and Don dropped his finger to the screen. "The whale! He's coming back. See!"

The pip was there again, indicating something coming down toward them. The whale had apparently gone to the surface, taken a few good breaths, and immediately started down again.

Don realized he'd sounded close to panic, as Shep whined and came against his legs. The dog was always sensitive to tones of his voice. To have apparently found the answer to their problem, and then have the whale decide to return, though . . .

"Kill the jets," Haller said. He sounded disgusted, but there was still no fear in his voice. "We'll sink faster without speed, and that's the best we can try now."

They were nearly eight hundred fathoms down—a trifle under a mile—when the whale drew above them. It came down, but it was obviously uncomfortable. Instead of a charge against the *Triton,* it slid down slowly, to nuzzle against the ship once, and then retreat. It started down after them again. For a second, it hesitated. Finally, reluctantly, at eight hundred and fifty fathoms, it gave up and rose before circling around and seeming to wait for them to come up again.

Don sighed at the end of that menace for the moment; it would at least have to return to the surface, which might give them a chance to ascend. He wondered again at nature's ability to handle problems that had baffled men for years; it had taken huge amounts of the finest alloys and careful design to permit the *Triton* to stand the pressure, but that big animal of simple flesh and bones could drop from the surface to a region where the pressure was over a ton to the square inch without apparently worrying.

"He must have high blood pressure down here," he commented. It wasn't much of a joke, but it brought enough of a laugh to ease some of the tension, and he felt better for it.

Haller had been speaking on the phone again. He cradled it now, and shrugged. "Torpedo tubes won't open at this pressure; I should have expected it. The *Triton* wasn't meant to carry them originally. And there isn't enough other weight we can eject. All the hatches were meant for escape, not for undersea dumping. Well . . ."

They were used to having Haller find a solution for

them by now, and waited for his next idea. But he shrugged at last.

"So we go down," he said. "Unless someone has ideas? No? All right, Don, try to spot the highest section of the bottom you think we can drift to, will you?"

Don noticed the use of his first name, and knew it was actually an admission that they were now under extreme emergency. Yet Haller seemed as unruffled as ever—until he came around to join Don in the search. Then the boy saw that the admiral's hands were sweating as much as his own, and noticed that there were tiny lines of strain around the man's eyes. Haller was worried and afraid too, but he had it under complete control, and wasn't losing his head. Don's respect for him rose again.

Upjohn stuck his head in then. The expression in his eyes showed that he was aware of the seriousness of the situation. His grin was a failure, though he managed to keep up a generally good act of normality. "Dexter and I've been busy keeping Kenney from tearing up the ship," he said. "We finally got him knocked out with a little force and some sleeping tablets. Anything we can do?"

"Thanks, nothing. Oh, tell the others we've decided to find a place on the bottom while we make repairs. That whale you felt made things pretty rough, but nothing we can't fix. And tell them what I said, Sid—not what you think I mean!"

"Right." The reporter went back quietly.

Haller turned back to the echo-sounder as Don grunted suddenly. The boy indicated what he had found. "There. It's about the highest point I've seen, and we might make it. Big enough, too."

"Twelve hundred fathoms—that's within our limits, from what I can find. About a ton and a half pressure to the inch." He nodded, and began giving directions to Cavanaugh.

The power came back on, at half speed. They shuddered and fluttered through the water, and Cavanaugh was having a rough time trying to compensate for the erratic behavior of the damaged diving plane and the stuck stern planes. They turned gradually until they were heading for the undersea plateau Don had spotted.

"Can you stand a little more?" Haller asked.

"Try," the helmsman said. The muscles bulged on his arms, but it was from strain rather than effort; the control motors were still working, doing the physical labor.

The ship increased its speed a trifle, and the fluttering and twisting grew worse. But now they were covering more distance for each foot they drifted downward. The plateau was nearer, but they were almost too low to make it.

"I can take a little more, sir," Cavanaugh forced out between clenched teeth. The deep brown of his skin seemed to be covered with tiny rhinestones of perspiration. At Haller's nod, he pushed the lever over a bit and hastily grabbed back at the wheel as the pitching threatened to get out of control.

It was going to be close. The edge of the plateau was a sharp cliff. If they missed the top, they would strike against that and go drifting down for thousands of feet more.

Then it was below them. They held their breath for a second, but there was no scraping or shock of collision.

"Kill the jets," Haller ordered.

Cavanaugh reached for the lever, and pushed it to STOP, but they continued drifting. Now there was a faint scraping sound from below. They began to relax, just as the helmsman shouted.

Ahead, and too small to have shown by echosounding, a single rock the size of several houses stuck up, and they were headed straight for it. There was more crunching against the bottom; then they barely had time to brace themselves for the collision before they hit.

It knocked Don over against his radar panel, and there was a terrific din. But most of their speed had been killed. He pushed himself back, saw that the others were all right, and let out a sigh of relief. They were still helpless, stranded where the pressure would be sure death at the least tiny leak, but there wasn't the lost feeling of drifting that they had known before.

Smoke suddenly reached his nose, together with a hissing sound. He jerked his eyes down and hastily ripped aside a panel of the set. With a groan, he yanked out a section of 600-ohm cable that had broken free on the impact and was shorting his power. But it was too late. The short had already burned out one section of his radio transmitter, leaving blackened resistors and melted connections mixed with the soft, waxy goo that had surrounded other parts.

"Better eject the antenna and send out a call for a rush job on a new diving plane," Haller began. Then he saw the mess of the transmitter. They could receive signals now, but there was no chance of sending any message from the ship.

"All right," he said. "So we'll have to make all repairs ourselves."

Don looked at his viewing panels, seeing the damaged diving plane outside. Fixing that from here was going to be a *real* problem!

CHAPTER 5 /

Men of the Sea

HALLER ASSEMBLED THE KEY MEN in the officer's wardroom to talk everything over before trying to start repairs. Don and his uncle were there, along with Drake, Walrich, Kayne and Upjohn.

Haller summed up the situation. As he saw it, they were lucky in a lot of ways. The *Triton* was standing the pressure with no sign of trouble, and they had no need to worry about air or power for their living needs. There were even supplies on board for at least six months. In the old days, a submarine on the bottom meant that it had to be rescued in a few hours or the men inside would suffocate. In their case, there was no immediate need to worry about the time repairs would take.

Simpson shook his head. "Afraid it isn't that good, sir. We can stay here quite a while, but I'd hate to risk it even for a month. There's a ton and a half of pressure on every square inch of hull. She can take it; she can take twice that for a short time, maybe. But even a ton wouldn't be safe indefinitely. When metal is under steady strain, the crystals of the alloys weaken—fatigue, we call it. Sooner or later, something will give—and we'd better not be here then!"

"I was coming to that," Haller agreed. "And men can only stand so much strain, too. In a month, some of us might very well crack under the emotional pressure, and that would be almost as disastrous. All right, we've got to get back to the surface as quickly as we can. That means repairing the tanks or the diving planes—preferably both. What about it?"

Drake looked at Walrich, who shrugged. The scientist made a disgusted grimace with his lips. "If we count on the tanks, we'll have to get outside to clean the valves. I was hoping the tar might have got inside—tar or whatever it is—and that dissolving some of it would free them. No results from the detergent, however. And doubling the engines on the valves strained the gears, but didn't budge them. As for the planes—well, it's the same situation. We'd have a hard time straightening the bow plane, even if we had it in our repair shop; but we can't touch it out there. All I know about the stern planes is that they won't respond."

"They stuck, just before the whale took after us," Kayne struck in. He was a slight, nervous man who always wore his cap to cover up his completely bald head, though he was only about twenty-five. "I was watching Cavanaugh when it happened. They just froze, with no warning. I'd like to get a good look at them."

"All right. Let's." Haller got up and started for the control room. "Will the packing glands on the periscope stand raising it. Dr. Simpson?"

Don's uncle grinned crookedly. "I wish the rest of the ship would hold as surely. The more pressure, the better they'll hold."

Don had never had a chance to look at the periscope in action before. It used a television remote pickup, too, instead of the old mirrors and prisms, but could be raised, tilted and turned to cover all directions. Haller reached for the controls, standing so the rest could see the big viewing screen that had replaced the tiny little opening of the old-style periscope. The big tube lifted easily for ten feet, while indicators threw cross-hatched lines over the image to show height and direction. He swung it to the bow diving plane first; it gave a better view than the bow pickup had done, showing that the plane was badly bent, but with no apparent damage to the hinge on which it swung.

"It'd be simple enough to get it off, if we were in shallow water," Simpson said. "Out there . . . Well, we've got a bathysuit on board that will stand any pressure the ship will. But working on that in the suit isn't going to be any picnic."

Haller's face cleared a little, though. Don remembered that he'd overlooked the bathysuit, which had been installed in a hatch after the plans had been first completed. It was a heavy steel ball, like a bathysphere, with just room inside for a man and an oxygen tank; but it was equipped with small caterpillar treads to move about and with grapples that could be controlled from inside, like arms. The trouble was that no grapple could be as skilful as a hand, and operating it was a continual backbreaking series of contortions.

The admiral swung the periscope to the rear, and began focusing on the stern diving plane. He frowned and adjusted it to show both rear planes. "What . . . ?"

Driven between the big planes and the tail assembly on both sides were two bright wedges that looked like copper! They looked as if they'd been designed to lock the planes, and had succeeded.

Drake recovered from the shock first. "Then I wasn't crazy. It was sabotage before. But how? Don't tell me your whale did that?"

"Somebody human, or something with a human being inside," Haller said grimly. "Something small and quiet enough to come up without our detecting him. Dr. Drake, when it happened to you, could it have been done at five hundred fathoms or more?"

Drake considered. "I guess so. We wouldn't have noticed it until we stopped diving, then, of course. I suppose so, yes."

"And this probably happened to us at about five hundred. Well, modern submarines can stand the pressure. And other bathysuits have been operated lower than that. Gentlemen, it looks as if someone doesn't want the *Triton* to succeed, and may be up there now, making sure we don't surface again. That would also account for the tarry material which apparently is jamming our valves."

It was the only explanation that seemed to fit, yet Don wondered about anyone in a bathysuit who could keep up with the *Triton*—even at half speed—and maneuver enough to remain out of sight of the pickups, make no sound, and also know exactly where to locate the ship, even when it was sailing under sealed orders. He saw his uncle stare at Drake; both of them also looked doubtful. Still, it was the only explanation they had.

And it wasn't a comfortable one.

Don moved to the sonar room, and began working the pickups, trying to explore the bottom around them. They were close to the edge of the clifflike drop that went down for thousands of feet further, he saw. Too close, in fact. The bottom sloped slightly, and it seemed that they were in constant danger of sliding slowly off.

Then he became aware that they had moved since landing. The ship was tilted slightly, as if it had rolled a few degrees toward the edge of the abyss below. And on the upper side, away from the cliff, there was a hollow in the soft bottom to show where they had first settled.

He looked at it sickly for a second before turning to call Haller. But the skipper had already guessed from his expression that something was up. Haller was at the screen at once, following Don's pointing finger. He studied the situation for a moment, and then began switching from pickup to pickup to get a better overall picture.

"I think we're all right," he decided. There was no need to tell the others. They had switched on the control screens, and were seeing it for themselves. "We slipped a little at first, but now we've dug in and settled enough that we should be all right. Of course, we don't know what it's like under this soft stuff here; if there's a steeper slope than there seems to be, the least thing might tilt us over and send us rolling down. But the rock we hit is still there, and it rolled a trifle when we struck—so I think we can forget that."

Yet he still stood studying the screens. Don got up, almost afraid to move for fear that the minute jar might upset the balance; Haller might think it was safe, but he couldn't know. Then he saw for himself what was worrying the skipper.

They had sunk into the soft mud enough to keep from sliding more, but also enough to hold them down to some extent; and the hollow their slipping had left was filling in as the soft stuff rolled down into the hole. If they continued to settle, they would reach a state where the mud would suck down on them and keep them from floating properly, even after repairs.

"We've got less time than I thought," Haller decided. "All right, we'll have to be out of here in forty-eight hours or so. But that still gives us time enough. If we can get a signal out, they can at least drop us a new diving plane. That will save repairs."

"We can do better than that," Simpson told him. "There are two more of these bathysuits back on the island, both bigger models than the one we carry. I meant to take them along when I was still hoping we'd use the *Triton* for oceanographic mapping. If we can send out a message, they can drop those down from above and handle the whole job."

Don looked at his uncle and then down at the wreck of the transmitter. He'd already checked the repair manual on the transmitter, and found that it was meant for normal troubles, and lacked the all-important information for a real rebuilding job. Still, there were replacements, and it could be fixed. He nodded doubtfully.

"I can fix it," he said. "But I don't know how long it will take."

Haller was also inspecting it. "We'll have to try. But the first thing we do is turn in and get some sleep. We'll save time in the long run and sometimes a fresh idea hits while a man's asleep. Don, you want to take first watch here? You can start in on this. I'll relieve you in four hours. This is about the only place where we need to keep a watch—on the screens."

"I'll stick with him," Upjohn volunteered. "I know enough about radio to hand him anything he needs, though that's about all."

Haller grinned. "I know a little more than that. Leave the routine stuff to me, and I'll solder your joints when I take over. Want some food sent in?"

Don settled down, studying the mess of the transmitter and keeping his eyes on the screens. Haller hadn't actually done a thing, or contributed a single idea. Yet somehow he gave the feeling of having everything in hand. And because of his presence, their chances were probably a lot better. He didn't look like a typical admiral—he was too stout, too short, and much too chubby-faced. But his calm voice and spotless suit lent him an air of confidence they needed, and it was clear that he knew how to get things done. Apparently that was what being a leader meant.

Upjohn pulled out a pencil and began chewing on it idly. He grinned toward the captain's stateroom, as if reading Don's thoughts. "Quite a guy, Bob Haller. I knew him when he was commanding an old-time sub in the war, which makes me older than I look, Don. When he came on, the crew hated him because he was replacing one of the real hero-type commanders. Haller never did anything you could call heroic, but he saved two big battlewagons, sneaked into a heavily mined harbor and wiped out a whole nest of the other side's subs, and then got depth-bombed trying to unsnarl a situation his superior had made a mess of. He brought the old ship back through enemy territory when any sane man would have known it couldn't travel ten knots under water. And never lost a man. When he left, his men acted as if the world had come to an end. . . . Well, what can I do to help?"

"Not much," Don admitted. "Keep Shep out of things, maybe."

The dog didn't like the smell of the burned parts, but

he was curious about all the work Don was trying to do, and kept sticking his head up to see what was going on. Upjohn laughed shortly, and pulled him away, while Don went ahead with the work.

The first job was to diagram all the layout that had been ruined. When he was sure he had it all down on paper, it would be safe to rip out the damaged section, but not until then. And since a few of the wires had come unsoldered, it was a matter of tracing and retracing circuits to be sure. This was work that would have been saved if the instruction manual had carried a complete schematic diagram, but that had somehow been omitted. From the fact that the list of transistors didn't check with the ones in the set, Don guessed that it was one of those cases where a model had been changed, and the manual revised hastily, with the idea of rewriting it later. He wondered how many men had lost their lives because somebody decided that such details weren't really important, and put off doing a good job until later.

Upjohn yawned after an hour of it, and stood up. "Gonna get me some coffee and walk around a bit. Want anything from the galley?"

Don shook his head. He glanced up at his screens, and switched to various pickups to keep an eye on things. But nothing seemed to have changed, except that the mud had filled in evenly around the *Triton* now.

He'd come to an experimental part of the rig now, where some engineer had discovered a new way to do things. He frowned over it and began pulling down books while he figured out the mathematics behind it, so that he could reconstruct the actual circuit. The work at college was coming in useful now.

Finally, he began tearing out all the ruined section. Since he had spare parts—something he'd checked carefully—it was simpler and faster to discard all this than to try to save whatever was still good. Shep suddenly growled, and Don glanced at him.

The dog was standing up, looking at the screen. Don glanced up at it, and saw something just sliding out of range, but was unable to make out any details. He frowned in surprise. While the screen gave a clear picture in colors as natural as could be expected through the water, he was surprised at Shep's reaction. Like most animals, the dog usually paid no attention to anything on a screen, apparently on the idea that if it didn't smell real, it was all nonsense. A few times before, he'd reacted to Don's uncle's face on the telephone panel from the office. He could recognize things when they interested him, apparently, but he usually didn't believe in them.

He must have been aware of the nervous tension on the ship, and ready to bark at anything.

Don went back to his work, only to hear another growl. This time he jerked his eyes directly up to the screen.

Swimming there in front of the pickup was a man! There was nothing unusual about the man, except for a seeming paleness to the skin and the odd clothes, that looked like a combination of a woman's ice-skating skirt and swimming trunk tops. But all around the man was a bubble. It didn't quite touch him anywhere, but was never more than half an inch from him. It seemed to be made of nothing but air, impossible as that was—or else of very thin cellophane. And on the back of the man was a small tank, which might contain more air.

Then another one swam into view, carrying a load of what looked like mud in his hands.

CHAPTER 6 /

Distress Signal

As HE WATCHED, Don saw the second swimmer come closer and heave the dark stuff in his hands. Then blackness settled onto the screen, just as Shep let out a sharp bark. Don stood with his mouth ajar for a second, then dived for the switch to change to another pickup. He heard Upjohn come into the room, but was too busy to look up.

He caught just a shadow in another pickup. Then the swimmers were gone.

"Did you see them?" he asked quickly, finally glancing at the reporter.

Upjohn looked puzzled. "I saw the screen go blank and saw you trying to get something on the pickup. What was it? It must have been good to make Shep react."

"It was," Don said. He told what he'd seen as factually as he could, trying to make it sound believable. But even with the knowledge that Drake and another had seen something of the same thing, he couldn't make it sound convincing to himself. Men simply couldn't exist without elaborate protection from bathyspheres or submarines at this depth; and air didn't form bubbles that fitted exactly the contours of a human being.

Upjohn didn't laugh, but he didn't seem excited, either. "I'm not saying you didn't see just what you said, Don," he decided. "I've seen things that couldn't exist before. One of the pictures that the experimental automatic rocket we sent out to Pluto brought back showed something that was obviously a piece of machinery. And no life of any advanced kind can live up there. But I've also seen some queer forms of life coming out of the ocean. You already heard Hawkes' story. And men just naturally see faces in clouds, and such things. Still—it must have looked darned close to human, if it wasn't. And there's that copper wedge out there in the diving plane."

He shrugged. "If we see 'em again, we'll yell out for the rest to come up. Otherwise report it to Haller later. What can we do about it if there *are* men out there, anyhow?"

When Haller came in to replace Don—looking as if he hadn't just gotten up—he listened, his face expressionless, and agreed with Upjohn. "No use writing it up in the log yet. I don't believe you saw such things, Don, but I don't think you're crazy or lying, either. Sid, where's your camera?"

Upjohn went out to get it, and came back, giving instructions on setting it so a picture could be taken from the screen. Haller set it beside him within easy reach, and went over Don's schematic and the work he had done on the set. "I'll stick to this section," he decided. "You handle the trick stuff, and I'll wire up the rest of it."

He ran a resistor wire through the hole in a socket, twisted it easily with needle-nose pliers, and touched it with the hot soldering iron, adding the smallest amount of solder. It was a beautiful job, and Don felt more confident. Haller had done electronic wiring before, obviously.

"I'll be back in four hours, Mr.—sir," Don said.

Haller grinned up at him as he marked off the work done on the diagram. "Make it Bob, Don. You're not bound to Navy regs, and I've been handing out first names already. Except when you're on duty—then we'll stick to the 'sir.' You're entitled to eight hours sack time—but if you want to cut it to four, I'll be grateful. Want me to buzz you?"

Don nodded. "Please," he said. He'd always been hard to wake, even with a full night's sleep, and he'd been wondering how he'd get up in time. The period between full sleep and really waking up always seemed too pleasant to give up.

But surprisingly, he was up when Haller buzzed him. Shep growled at the signal, and then relaxed as he heard Haller's voice. He was an obedient dog, but ships imposed strains on his habits; anything more than a small sailboat was foreign territory to him, except as something men kept at the docks to make interesting smells.

Haller had done a remarkable amount. Except for the experimental section—the part with the circuit that had given Don the trouble before—it was finished. The boy took over, twisting the coils around coil-forms of plastic he had stripped. He could only hope they would work; coil tables told how they should be wound, but any time a man followed such a table and got exactly what he wanted, he put it down as a minor miracle. Haller finished them with coil dope and tinned the leads as Don completed them.

"Wish I had a Q-meter," Don complained. "We're a little limited on test equipment. I'll have to check it all with a signal generator and meter, I guess."

He stayed at it while Haller began picking up the business of getting repairs under way, as the rest of the men got up.

From the wardroom, he heard the querulous voice of Senator Kenney complaining. There was the sound of the man's feet stamping toward the control room, and more angry words. Don strained his ears, but he couldn't make out what Haller told him. Apparently, it was a short course on the events that had happened.

"And you didn't waken me? You let Dexter and that upstart reporter lock me up while that was going on? Admiral Haller, I might have been killed! When I report this . . ."

"Not at all," Haller said, and this time his voice was plainer. "If we had been about to die, I'd have had you wakened, Senator. I've always felt that no man should die in his sleep if he doesn't want to."

"Hmm." The Senator thought that one over, apparently, and decided to ignore any possible sarcasm. "Well, what's done is done. And you say we'll soon be able to communicate?"

Don heard the panel slide back, and looked up to see the Senator's gray face. The man looked in and nodded slowly. "Go right ahead, young man. Don't stop anything that will get us out of this situation." His voice was curiously subdued. "Admiral, I—I'm not used to this sort of thing. I find it—well, I find it somewhat shocking. I confess, I feel somewhat sick. I think I'll retire. I—uh—thank you, Admiral. Thank you, young man."

He staggered out of the control room, no longer a man who could make and break others, but a beaten, tired old man who saw signs of danger he was untrained to meet or even understand. When talk failed to settle things, he had nothing else to fall back on. He probably was the same man underneath as he had been thirty years before, when his name had been on so much of the legislation that was still studied in schools as a model of good government. But too many years had passed with people around who bowed to his slightest wish, and the Senator had no real contact with the world outside of his own narrow sphere. Maybe he knew he hadn't kept up, and that added to his bitterness.

Don shrugged these thoughts off, and dug the voltmeter and signal generator out of the kit. The signal generator was a small, portable one. It had tiny batteries to power it, and a pair of the new aluminum-antimony transistors to generate the signal. By varying the setting, a tiny radio signal of any frequency between a hundred kiloherz and five hundred megaherz could be produced. Don switched it on and tested it quickly, setting it for an audio modulation. This added a four hundred cycle beat to the regular signal. The four hundred cycles raised and lowered the amount of the high-frequency radio signal four hundred times a second, of course—and he could strip it back off with a tiny crystal and pair of headphones, to give him an audible test of how it was going.

He coupled on the generator, set it to the proper frequency, and began testing the circuit with the meter. Then he stuck the generator into his shirt pocket and began checking voltages.

Everything seemed to be in order, except that the signal barely crept through, where it should have been amplified thousands of times. He puzzled over the circuits, while he heard Haller, Drake, Walrich and his uncle conferring. The ship was busy as men went about trying everything that they could think of.

Repairs of the transmitter had gone much faster than he had expected, but obviously the others weren't waiting on him. They were hoping he could get a message out, so that nobody would have to go out in the bathysuit, but they weren't counting on it. Maybe it was a good thing, too—certainly the set seemed as useless as before.

Then, as he tapped an electrolytic condenser in the tricky section, the meter suddenly jumped. An intermittent! A part that seemed to be in good condition, but went off and on, sometimes acting one way when "loaded" with the meter and another way in normal operation.

He yanked it out and soldered in another. And this time, the signal built up a step at a time as it should, until it reached the main transmitter section, which was still in good condition. The new coils weren't quite right, but a few trial squeezings and spreadings settled that; it wasn't perfect, but it would work properly.

He called in Haller, but didn't wait to eject the antenna buoy and began letting it unreel toward the surface. The buoy collapsed violently as the pressure hit it—he could follow that from a nearby pickup—but it was filled with helium and designed to collapse without losing the power to float. The thin, insulated wire began rising steadily.

Haller clapped him on the back. "Good work, Don. Here, I've had the message written out for hours. It'll give them enough dope to proceed with caution and watch out for whatever jammed those planes. Keep sending until they locate the buoy."

It might take hours for an accurate fix, Don knew. But now there was hope again inside the ship. Finally an automatic signal came back down the wire to indicate it had surfaced. He pulled the key to him and began sending the dots and dashes of an SOS.

The little antenna, so far above, was the best that could be designed for the purpose, but it wasn't too efficient. Lying so close to the surface of the ocean, it was capable of sending out only a limited signal. If someone were listening for it, and conditions were good, the answer might come at once. Otherwise, he'd have to keep trying.

He cut off after five minutes, and began listening across the dial. The receiver could operate better, since it was hunting for a signal pumped out by the huge shore installations, with kilowatts of power and whole buildings of equipment; anyhow, even a small receiver could amplify by millions of times a signal picked up.

He caught a rapid flash of Spanish, and started to turn on. But Haller bent closer, twisting one of the phones to his ear. "Storm up above," he translated. "That's the big government job sending out storm warnings to all small craft. The storm we saw coming must have hit. Waves . . . Uh! We're right in the hurricane path, if they're correct. There it comes in English."

Don heard it through, groaning. It was coming in with a heavy surge, fading to nothing, and then blasting out again. The little antenna must be bobbing about, under water a lot of the time. It was completely waterproofed, but it couldn't operate normally under such conditions. It must be really pitching on the surface!

He tried again, listened, and then again. There was no answer. He shifted down to the lowest frequency his set could handle, where there would be less chance of the beaming effect keeping it from spreading the maximum distance. And still there was no answer.

Then an answer came, faint and almost inaudible. Obviously, judging by the hand-operated keying, it was from some ship, rather than from one of the big installations. From the words he got, he gathered that they were asking what they could do.

"Have them relay," Haller instructed.

Don sent instructions, and repeated the message. This time he got more of the answer as the operator checked back. They were having trouble receiving him. Only part of his message was complete.

There was more, too. He read it off to Haller as it came through. ". . . Sorry can't do better. Bad shape ourselves. Edge of hurricane got us. We're sinking fast, waiting arrival rescue ship. Will send what we have, then must contact rescue ship. Will . . ."

Then it cut down to a faint trickle of sound, and was suddenly gone. Don shook his head. From the sound of things, and the erratic keying, the operator up there was in a lot worse trouble than he was. He had a picture of the man, sitting pounding at his key while he heard the shouts of the men on his ship as the water rose higher and higher, and the ship probably began to break up under the pounding of the waves. In the middle of his desperate attempts to keep in touch with the rescue ship, he'd taken time out to answer another SOS and relay what he could of the message. Don had no idea of how close that rescue ship might be, but he made a hasty, silent prayer that it would arrive in time.

He began searching and sending again, alternately, trying to make another contact. He heard bits of totally useless chitchat. And then a strong signal came through, in precise, machine Morse, obviously beamed with the full power of a land station.

"Calling *Triton.* Relay message received, incomplete. We are attempting to get a fix, will despatch destroyer for bathysuits—query bathysuits?—earliest possible and proceed to location. Set transmitter to frequency. . . ."

It cut off abruptly, without warning. Don checked his receiver, and then began tuning again. But now there was no message of any sort coming in. He cut in the transmitter, and a meter dipped suddenly, indicating something wrong, as if his antenna were disconnected.

A sudden sickening sensation ran through him. He cut on the pickup that covered the section where the antenna wire had run out, and pressed the rewind button. The wire was almost invisible, even under the lights that bit through the thick water, but he could just make it out as it bobbed downward under the slightly unsteady force of the reel.

After about five hundred feet had been reeled in, it came to an end. There was nothing more. The wire had parted. Somewhere up above, their only antenna buoy floated on the lashing waves of a hurricane, no longer connected. There was now no way in which they could send a signal for the needed fix.

And without that, the Navy might hunt for weeks without locating them. The buoy would drift for miles, even if it could be located. To make matters worse, there was a storm raging which might not abate for days, and sonar traces from this depth would be useless.

CHAPTER 7 /

Repair Task

"CUT!" HALLER EXCLAIMED. "Don, I'm almost ready to believe in those bubble men everyone has been seeing!"

Don jerked back from his bitter thoughts to even grimmer ones. Haller was right. The line couldn't have broken. Not at five hundred feet up. The reel was set to soak up all normal shocks—even such ones as might be produced by the waves above. And if the wire had broken under strain, it would have broken near the top, where there would have been more snap, rather than so far down that all the pitching had long since been absorbed.

It looked as if something had deliberately severed the line. And since the wire was a tough alloy of copper and beryllium, it must have taken some cutting; an alloy like that could cut steel, or stand more bending than the best phosphor bronze—not to mention the protection of the rugged plastic insulation.

It couldn't have been the whale, either, even if the creature had teeth with which to bite, which it did not. The whale had stayed up a good deal higher than that. He'd spotted it on the sonar screen, high above, not too long before. He was sure that this wasn't the explanation. There were also a number of monstrous creatures swimming about outside, some that looked as if they had evolved from lobsters, except that their pinchers had great flaming bunches of hairlike material growing from them, shining phosphorescently as most of the life forms did down here. But they had shown no interest in the wire, and certainly couldn't have cut through it without giving some warning on the strain signal.

Haller called Drake and Simpson up, and reported the situation. "We'll have to go out," he said finally. "The bathysuit is our only hope now. Is it ready?"

"It's been ready for hours," Drake told him. "And we've attached the tools that should be needed. Ed and I have pretty well worked out the way of tackling the job, too, but I haven't convinced him yet that I'm the one to do the job."

He grinned at Don's uncle, who grinned back. But Haller shook his head. "Neither one of you will do it. This is a job for the best man, not for volunteers. That means a young man—even half an hour in that thing is tough going—and someone who's small enough to have a better chance of moving around in it."

"I'm ready," Don told him. The words came out, but he wasn't sure that he meant them. The idea of being down here in the *Triton* was bad enough, but the ship was so much a world in itself that he didn't think too much about it, most of the time. But to go out in that pressure, with only the small bathysuit . . .

Haller stared at him thoughtfully. "I was thinking of Kayne. But you're right. You're younger than any of us, so you're probably more adjustable and have better reflexes. And you're shorter than Kayne—and a lot slimmer than I am. All right, you've got the job."

Simpson started to protest at having his nephew take the risk, and then nodded slowly. All things considered, Don was the logical candidate for the job.

The machine shop had been crammed in under the torpedo-control room, and the bathysuit was in a small hatch just off that. Properly speaking, it wasn't really a hatch. The bathysuit fitted exactly into it, with almost no spare space; there was an outer section that could be opened to let the suit out, and an inner screw-type seal that permitted entrance directly into the top of the bathysuit globe, and could be closed then to keep the ship watertight under the terrific pressure.

That was open now, in line with the screw top of the globe, which had also been opened. Inside the bathysuit was a cluster of controls which would direct the treads underneath it or the grapple-arms at the side. There were also batteries and an oxygen tank, together with a small lithium-hydroxide arrangement for removing the carbon dioxide from the air.

Haller, Drake and Simpson went over the plans with Don. The first job would be to remove the wedges from the stern diving planes; after that, he was to remove the whole damaged bow plane and put it into the hatch. That would then be blown out, and men would go to work on it frantically while he cleaned out the valves on the tanks as best he could. If they were lucky, they'd be able to pass the bow plane out again before he had to come back.

He had air in the bathysuit for an hour and a quarter. Under no conditions was he to stay out more than an hour. "No heroics," Haller cautioned him. "We don't want to lose you—and remember that the suit is the only one we have. If you endanger yourself, you endanger that—and all of us. No matter what happens, don't stay out one second beyond the hour mark. I'd rather have a man who takes precautions and follows necessary orders than a man who could swim to the surface with the whole *Triton* on his back, fighting off monsters all the way. Heroism is a wonderful thing, when it's done for a good reason and with intelligence. But foolhardiness wins medals only half the time—the rest of the time, it ruins everything."

Don blushed. He'd been thinking that he'd stay as long as he possibly could if necessary; he'd been suppressing his worry about going out by imagining their tribute when he staggered back at the last second, having saved them all at the risk of his life. But Haller's words made sense.

He had been in the bathysuit once before, when it had first been completed, and he was fairly familiar with the controls, which meant he could make it move about where he wanted and could locate the grapple controls. He went over them now with his uncle, trying to memorize everything, and to make sure he knew how to locate and handle the various wrenches and other tools.

Finally he climbed into the interior of the "head" of the bathysuit and settled into place. He had to fit into a cramped space, with his legs bent up and his back against the curved, padded wall. A tiny pickup on top could be swiveled around to reveal his surroundings outside on a small screen in front of his eyes, and a telephone connection to the ship snapped over his ears and throat. In theory, his legs were free enough to operate the tread controls, leaving his hands for the grapples; the pickup was controlled by motions of his head.

His uncle clasped his shoulder briefly, and then the top began to screw in. All sounds vanished, except the hissing of the tiny air-purifying machinery. His stomach knotted up in a ball, and he felt his lungs begin laboring at the tightness that cut him off from everything Sweat popped out on his forehead. But after a few seconds, it passed. He still felt uncomfortable, and he was sorry he'd ever volunteered. But now was no time to back out.

Suddenly he heard a heavy crash, and realized that the valves must have been opened, letting in the water outside. The inner seal would be closed, except for a narrow air valve that would bleed off the air as the sea rushed in. Then it was over.

"Okay, roll her out," Drake's voice said in his ears. "And take it easy at first. We're a little doubtful of that power cable that connects you with the ship's generators. If you see your lights flicker, pull back that red lever: You'll be on battery power then, and you'll have just ten minutes in which to get back."

Don watched, but there seemed to be no trouble. He maneuvered the controls with his feet, and there was a faint feeling of movement as the suit backed out. In the panel, he could see himself passing out of the compartment in the ship. A minute later, he was moving over the mud of the bottom, with the ship between him and the cliff.

The mud was soft, but it supported him on the wide treads. He rolled along slowly, keeping a careful watch on the power cable that stretched out behind. He'd have to be careful not to let that kink.

Now that he was moving, he was less aware of the pressure around him; he began to feel almost like some weird undersea creature. He moved back carefully until he was beside the diving plane. The ship had settled more in the rear here, and he found that he could just reach over the top of it; he'd expected to have to use the grapples to pull himself up onto it.

The copper wedge showed up plainly now in the light that streamed out from just under his pickup. He got two of the "hand" grapples onto it finally, and began working at it. It had been driven in tightly, but was soft enough for him to work on. Slowly at first, he wiggled it about. A minute later, it came out—a simple wedge of copper. He dropped it and moved around to the other side.

Here the plane was higher off the mud, and he had to pull himself up, using four of the grapples. There was a faint sound of groaning from the motors built into the shell, but they lifted him slowly, until he could inch along the plane itself. This was the tricky part, since a slip might throw him off and onto his side. He could right himself with the grapples, but it would be a tedious and slow job.

With better leverage, however, the wedge came out more quickly. He reported back over the phone, and began letting himself down—a lot more difficult job than lifting himself had been. There was little work involved, since the motors took care of that, but the strain of manipulating the controls left him sweating again, faster than the air conditioning could soak up the moisture.

"Stern diving planes are working again," Drake reported. Don swung the pickup back and saw that the planes were tilting up and down. Now, if anything should happen and the ship were to slip off, there would be a faint chance of climbing back.

He worked back around to the bent plane, watching his power line carefully. This time he couldn't climb up. He had to stand on the mud, moving about a little to keep from sinking, and reach up to work the grapples and try to remove the plane.

Getting a wrench into just the right position proved to be worse than anything he'd tried yet. He got it onto the big nut, finally, and began working on it. The wrench had a motor-driven action, geared down, but it threatened to lift him from his treads as it went to work. Then he realized it was because he didn't have it fully on, where another section would hold it firmly, giving him the full benefit of the motor drive. With the clumsy grapples, it took another two minutes to get the wrench properly placed.

The weight of the diving plane put a strain on the power of the suit, but he got it off finally and lugged it back to the hatch. He forced it in, muttering unhappily as he found that it had never been designed to fit. Finally, though, he managed to find a way of making it go in far enough for the outer seal to close.

As soon as he reported the job done, the hatch closed and the pumps began to drive out the water so men could open the inner seal. But Don didn't stay to watch. He still had the valves to take care of, and it was becoming increasingly plain that the tanks would have to be drained to float the *Triton*. She was still settling deeper into the ooze.

He had begun working on the valve ports for the bow trim tanks when his uncle reported that they had maneuvered the big diving plane into the ship. "Pretty bad shape," Simpson said. "We won't be able to do a good job, but I guess we can straighten it enough to work for a while. How's it coming out there?"

"The valve looks as if someone had deliberately stuffed it with that tarry stuff," Don reported. "It's hard as iron, too, and seems to be glued to the metal." He was trying to chip out a hole in it, but the pick wouldn't touch it. The detergent might have softened it, but the ocean would have diluted that too quickly.

"Must be the temperature; it softened up enough to wash away by itself before when the *Triton* reached the surface—if it's the same stuff." Simpson paused, and Don could hear him talking to someone else for a minute, though he couldn't make out the words. Then he spoke into the phone again. "We're putting the underwater welding torch through to you. Try to warm it up with that."

Don lumbered back to the hatch, just as it opened. Inside, he found the torch and its cable, and turned back to the trim-tank valve again. It was a good thing he'd stuck his nose into everything during the assembling of the *Triton;* he even had a little experience with the welder.

He cut it on and turned the glaring spot of concentrated heat on the black stuff in the valve. The torch didn't work as well at this pressure as it would have done further up, but it apparently gave out enough heat for the job. The tarry substance suddenly began to soften rapidly and to dribble out of the valve, dissolving as it went.

He cleaned it out as thoroughly as he could and went on to the others. His body ached from the cramped position, and it was getting harder all the time to control the steering with his feet. But he cleaned out the valves, one by one. To get at some of them meant standing between the edge of the abyss and the ship; he worried about it every second there, but nothing happened.

Finally he reported back, and headed for the hatch. The big diving plane was just finished, they told him, and was being put through the hatch. Then he saw the outer seal open, and moved up to begin removing the plane. It came out easier than it had gone in. He saw that it was nearly straight now, with evidence of hasty pounding and welding. It didn't look like a good job, but there was nothing to be done about that now; it was probably as good as they could do with the limited facilities of the ship.

Then he glanced at his watch. "Time's up," he reported. "I'm still okay on air, according to the tank valve, and I feel fairly good. I might be able to install the plane in the time left. But . . ."

"Good man," Haller's voice answered quickly. "You've got one minute left, to be exact. All right, Don, since you're keeping your head and following orders, I guess it's safe. Take twelve minutes more. Then get back here, no matter what happens."

Don sighed with relief at not having to go through the process of getting out and then back into the suit again. He picked up the diving plane and towed it along to the bow. Getting it in place was tricky, but by now he'd learned how to control the grapples better. And this time, he knew enough to use the big motorized wrench properly.

He still had four minutes of air left when they tested the plane and decided he had done all he could.

Then, as he turned back to the hatch, he saw the men in bubbles again. This time, there were a dozen of them. Some were equipped with something like pots of the black tar, and three held wedges of copper. They waited, swimming about lazily a mere fifty feet beyond him.

"Captain Haller!" he shouted into his phone.

But Haller answered before he could report. "I know. We can see your bubble men this time. But there's nothing you can do. Get back on board!"

CHAPTER 8 /

Battle Below

AS HE STEPPED INTO THE HATCH, Don saw the bubble men begin to swim forward. They moved easily, turning to circle around the ship. For the first time, he saw that each wore a maze of tanks and small machinery on his back, with what must be weights scattered about to balance him and to keep him from floating upward.

Then the seal on the hatch closed, and his view was cut off. He could hear Haller shouting quick orders, the sounds coming faintly through his phones. But he had to wait what seemed hours, while the water was forced out of the hatch, and the inner seal opened. Then there was the delay of getting the seal on his bathysuit unscrewed. The warning light blinked just before that came off, indicating his air supply was nearly exhausted.

Simpson and Haller helped him out of the suit. Don found that his muscles were so cramped that he could hardly stand for the first few steps. But with fresh circulation, his legs began to function again.

"They're trying to jam the planes and block the valves," he gasped out.

Haller nodded grimly. "I know. We're watching this time, so they can't sneak up on us. They can't make that tar work while the trim tanks are being drained; the outgoing water would wash it away. And Cavanaugh's

61

keeping the diving planes moving as fast as they'll go, so it should be a little hard to block them. Did you see anything to show what nationality they might be?"

"No—they didn't even look like anyone I've seen," Don told him. "No nation could be that advanced, sir!"

They were moving back toward the bridge. Don slipped into his sonar room, to relieve Upjohn, while Haller stood staring at the instruments on the control panel. "They're not Martians!" the admiral said, but his voice didn't sound too sure. In the screens, the bubble men were swimming about busily. One drew near one of the valves with some of the black stuff, but from his expression as he moved off, it was plain that the tar hadn't stuck.

"Bottom ooze is still sucking at us," Cavanaugh reported. "We seem to be stuck, sir."

"We'll reach flotation in a second," Haller said confidently. Almost on his words, the *Triton* seemed to lurch a trifle. "Keep pumping."

Simpson had come up, and now shook his head quickly. "Not too much flotation! We've got to go up slowly. The hull's been under pressure for hours. Too fast a release might put more strain on her than she'll stand."

"Cut the pumps to minimum, run them every other minute," Haller ordered promptly. "That should be enough to keep their tar from sticking. Ah!"

The *Triton* had stirred weakly. Now she began to come up, and suddenly seemed to leap sharply. Haller issued quick orders for the main tanks to be opened. They rose rapidly for a few seconds, and then slowed as the intake of water increased their weight to nearly that of the sea water they displaced. Haller set the pumps to working alternately, taking in water and then ejecting it.

Outside, the bubble men were apparently in conference. Two of them started for the ship with the copper blocks. The *Triton* lurched sickly as Cavanaugh started wiggling the diving planes. At this depth, the pressure of the steam and water coming from her big atomic jets was largely neutralized by the outside pressure, and the ship was sluggish. But the maneuver was enough to discourage the men outside. Don watched them confer again—then swim off.

"They're going down!" he reported, in surprise. He'd expected them to rise toward some ship which must be higher up.

Haller nodded, but made no comment. He was watching the instruments as the men rose cautiously.

Don suspected a trick, and began scanning carefully with all pickups and the full sonar equipment. But the bubble men had gone. And he could get no pip indicating a ship above. Even the whale seemed to have given up and gone elsewhere.

The bow diving plane that had been hastily welded didn't work perfectly. Obviously, it still caused some turbulence in the water, and kept Cavanaugh busy correcting. But navigation was possible now. The *Triton* was nearly a hundred fathoms off the bottom and rising steadily in a wide spiral. Haller stopped the emergency work on the pumps, and had the ship balanced against her displacement and carefully leveled off with the trim tanks. She began acting more normally, now that the strain was taken off the diving planes.

Upjohn came back, standing lazily in the doorway and chewing on a toothpick. "Kenney's gone back to bed," he told Don. "He's sick again. I told him about the bubble men, and he's expecting them to drop an atomic depth charge on us, or something. He took a batch of sedatives. Maybe I should do the same. I'm going nuts trying to figure out how those men can get down this far in those things—and why. If any nation has a scientific development like that, what do they care about the *Triton*? She'd be kindergarten stuff to them."

"Get the pictures off the screens?" Haller asked.

The reporter nodded. "I developed a few. The negatives show enough details, unless someone decides they're darkroom fakery. I wish I'd gotten a better group shot, though."

Don ran through the pickups again, and turned back to the sonar screen. He frowned at what he saw, and again tried the viewing panel connected to the pickups. This time he could make out enough to be sure.

"You'll have a chance," he told Upjohn. "They're coming back!"

At the limits of the distance they could scan, a group of the bubbles had appeared. Don couldn't count the number exactly, but there seemed to be more than the dozen men who had surrounded the *Triton* before. And with them was a larger bubble, glowing very faintly in the darkness of the water around it.

"Full speed ahead!" Haller ordered quickly.

The *Triton* had been moving along lazily. Now she jumped ahead. Surprisingly, at full speed the turbulence which had bothered them from the imperfections of the bow diving plane seemed to smooth out. Cavanaugh reported steering normal, and widened the spiral in which they were rising.

But the sea men came on steadily. They were close enough now for Don to make out more details, and he pointed to one who was in advance of the others. The bubble man wasn't swimming, this time; instead, he was lying on a thin, flat object which seemed to be something like a surfboard. Two small propellers at the front were lashing the water, and pulling the whole device along at a speed considerably better than the *Triton* could make. It was as if the bubbles offered no resistance to the sea.

Kayne snorted. "Using propellers as tractors. Who'd do a thing like that?"

"Somebody who knows more about conditions down here than we do," Haller said crisply. "Not entirely dumb, either. There'd be better control that way. And the force of the slip stream doesn't seem to bother them. They must have ridden those things when they came up to us for the sabotage before."

"While the whale took up all our attention," Upjohn agreed. "I'd say we're dealing with some smart people, whoever they are. I wonder what other gadgets they've got up their sleeves?"

Haller frowned, and ordered Cavanaugh to take the

ship up faster. They began rising more steeply. But the men outside seemed not to notice. They also rose, still shortening the distance. And now Don could see that each had something like a rope in his hands, with one end fastened to the front of the board he rode.

The sea men drew up alongside the *Triton,* and the ropes suddenly shot out sharply. At the end of each was a cone of what seemed to be metal, and it was this which tipped him off to the idea. He chuckled sharply, bringing Haller's eyes around. The admiral smiled wryly. They'd have a hard time making the trick work. The weights must be magnets, designed to stick tightly to the hull of the *Triton;* but the alloys of which the hull was made were nonmagnetic.

The sea men became aware of that a second later. Don had one in clear focus on the screen, and he could see the surprise run over the pale features. The man stared at the metal piece he had recovered, then glanced around at his companions.

They drew back for a second, before coming in again. This time, the throwing was repeated, but with no attempt to touch the hull of the *Triton.* The cords went over the top of the ship. On the side opposite the throwers another group was waiting. Don switched from one pickup to another, and saw the opposite group catching the ends of the ropes and fastening them quickly to the boards they rode.

Haller frowned. "Blow the tanks," he ordered. "And take her up!"

Cavanaugh began bringing the bow of the *Triton* up, just as the men on the boards started to circle around the ship, trying to wrap their ropes firmly around her. As soon as they saw the ship tilt, they began to concentrate on the bow of the *Triton.* The ropes should have slipped off the smooth hull, but instead they clung tightly; somehow, they had an impossible holding power. They stuck as firmly as the suckered arm of an octopus. Don wondered whether they might not have something similar to the suction cups built into them, on a tiny scale.

Now there were nearly twenty of the men with their motorized boards attached to the ship, and they began to exert their full force downward. They had power far in excess of their appearance, too. The ship came back to even keel, then began to head downward.

Haller was staring at the screen, and the skin around his eyes had whitened with strain. "The one fault with this ship," he said tautly. "You can reverse a propeller, at least. But . . ."

Don stared at him in surprise. Then he realized that Haller had never been given a thorough briefing on the ship, and that the papers given him by the Navy had been so bulky he couldn't have read all the fine print— and that some of the most important features probably were treated as things to be passed over quickly. He was beginning to realize that an engineer couldn't look at a ship in the same light as a skipper must.

They'd never gotten around to installing a reverse stop on the indicator, either. There were probably a lot of things like that on this model.

"The jets work either way," he said.

Haller didn't waste time on surprise. He picked up the phone to the engine-control room and signaled frantically. "Reverse engines," he ordered when Drake must have answered. "Full speed astern."

They were bucking against the ropes one second. The next, the ship heaved violently. Reversal here could be done in almost no time. Don saw the sea men on the screen look back in shock and then move wildly aside as the superheated jets kicked out through the ocean ahead. The heat would be dissipated almost at once, but it still must have seemed horrible to them. They broke free, throwing off their ropes, and began getting out fast.

It was a good thing for them, too. The jets of water that shot out of the engines weren't just hot in temperature; they were hot from a radiation point of view. In going through the engines, they picked up a definite radioactive charge. There was no reason to try to keep from contaminating the water—in the great mass of the ocean, a million *Tritons* could have operated for thousands of years without raising the general radioactivity level enough to matter. But at close hand, long contact with the jets could have been fatal.

The *Triton* shot backward, still trailing the ropes. Then her bow came up again, and Haller called for full speed ahead. She was rising now, faster than had seemed safe. But they had to take chances. The sea men were already reforming and getting ready for some other move.

It came suddenly from above. Don saw one of the men outside look up, and shifted his pickup to one that would cover the water overhead. He'd noticed that the sonar was absolutely useless against the bubbles; even at close range, there was no response from the sound-echo device.

On the screen of the television hookup was the big bubble he had seen from a distance, keeping pace with the *Triton* and exactly above it. Men in bubbles were driving their rafts toward it. As he looked, he saw one move up to the big bubble and apparently fade through it and inside, where there were bulky objects of some sort.

A moment later, the man came diving down again, bringing with him one of the objects. It seemed to be a large rock, except that the bottom had been ground smooth.

"Hard a-lea!" Haller ordered. The *Triton* swung sharply, taking off at an angle. They had been spiraling toward the port side, and the course was a reversal of their previous one.

But the rock was obviously being guided with sufficient power to keep up. It stayed overhead, coming down steadily. A few seconds later, it struck just ahead of the conning-turret section. It landed exactly over one of the pickups, and Don had a last second view of the bottom of the stone, equipped with small cups in something that resembled the tar he had seen before. The effect was similar to the suction cups on an octopus, as he had suspected.

He swung to another pickup as the screen went dark, and saw that the rock was being detached from a larger sled that had guided it down. Above it, another one was coming.

Cavanaugh was already having a difficult time trying to keep the *Triton* operating properly, with the added weight toward the bow and the turbulence of the water set up by the rock.

Haller glanced at the screen again, and nodded slowly. "Ram them if you can," he ordered.

Cavanaugh set the screen in front of him, and brought the ship around in a surprisingly smooth maneuver, considering the rock resting on her. Ahead lay a group of the bubble men on their boards. He lined them up and began heading for them, driving the ship at full speed.

The move must have been unexpected. The sea men looked back just as the *Triton* came bearing down on them at her top speed. Don saw one of them open his mouth in surprise. Then the *Triton* hit.

The men in the bubbles were tossed aside instantly, while the *Triton* ploughed through the space where they had been. Don felt sick, but he switched to a rear pickup. He brought his eyes back to the screen reluctantly—and let out a surprised cry as he saw what lay behind.

The bubble men had not been hurt. They had been pushed aside, but those odd, fragile looking bubbles had taken the full impact of the *Triton* without a sign of strain. Behind, the bubble men were re-forming, and one of them was grinning savagely toward the ship.

Then the second rock hit the ship.

CHAPTER 9/

Captured!

THREE OTHER ROCKS came down almost at the same time. The *Triton* dipped and lurched as the weights altered her balance. She threatened to turn over, and Don grabbed at his control board, his stomach twisting inside him. Cavanaugh and Kayne were working frantically, with a flurry of words that were mixed up with the sharp, quick orders of Haller.

Somehow, Kayne managed to get the trim tanks adjusted in time, while Cavanaugh fought and won the battle of holding the *Triton* upright by using the diving planes and rudders.

Haller gave orders to blow the tanks completely, and the main ballast tank pump began working. The speed of the descent changed, until they were settling slowly. But they could not rise, even with the full power of the jets driving the ship forward on diving planes that were set to force her upward.

"Locates that plateau, Mr. Miller," Haller ordered. "We'll have to land there again."

Don began a frantic search, to find that by some accident they were exactly over the spot from which they had taken off. He tracked down a spot that should be just beyond the place where they had first landed, further from the edge of the abyss. He called out the coordinates.

They came down in a tight spiral. And now the sea people seemed content to let them land with no further trouble. The whole maneuver appeared to be aimed at keeping them on the bottom, rather than in doing them any actual direct harm. The men in the bubbles came riding down alongside. Most of them had sent their odd sea sleds up to the big bubble, and were swimming along casually on their own power.

They landed about fifty feet from the hole in the muck of the bottom which marked the original site. This time there was no trouble. They found a flat place, with no tilt, and drifted down to it, to land with almost no shock. Haller nodded quick approval at Cavanaugh.

"Coffee," he said, and it was an order. They moved back to the wardroom where the steaming pot was always full. Don hadn't seen the cook since they had first left the island. He had a mental picture of a little man scurrying about nervously, making coffee and sandwiches, afraid of his own shadow, and never looking at another man. He was a little surprised to see the lean, short man standing there, grinning out of a mouth that had a big scar twisted across it and up his face.

"How's it going, skipper?" he asked, touching his forelock.

Haller grinned at him, and slapped his back roughly. "Not so good, Ham. Looks as if you won't be able to retire, after all. We're in the brig."

"We'll get out, somehow," the little man said. He grinned at Don. "Best skipper in the Navy, kid—or out of it. Shipped out together, we did, first time—before skipper made Annapolis the hard way. When you gonna eat a decent meal, skipper?"

"Later, Ham, later." Haller grinned after him as he went back to the galley, and then his face sobered. "I wish I believed him. Getting out of this doesn't look so good."

He turned as Upjohn came in with Simpson and Drake behind him. Don stared at his uncle, and sudden pride washed over him. Simpson looked worried, but there was no real fear there. Drake showed some signs of being afraid; he was licking his lips nervously and running his hands over his hair as if to dry them. But both seemed far more worried about the ship than about themselves.

They talked it over, dropping all formality and going back to first names. Dexter came in, lifting an eyebrow to Haller. His face sagged at Haller's shrug, but he took the bad news like a soldier. He sat down quietly, listening, but not saying much of anything. His eyes were busy studying them, but his attitude was that of a man who knew he could do nothing and was willing to wait for those who could to decide. Don knew very little about him, but liked what he saw.

The cook bustled about, setting the table for them and trying to get them to sit down. He'd cooked up a hasty meal of canned bacon and frozen eggs, scrambled. Don dropped into a chair and sampled it, his appetite whetted by the odor. Then he fell to on it, while the others gradually followed his example.

They had few suggestions to make, and those few came to nothing. The idea of using the jets, alternating between forward and reverse rapidly, was the best. The *Triton* might bob back and forth under the kicking of power, but not too much, with low power. And the hot liquid from the jets was supposed to rise over the hull and heat the tarry stuff on the rocks until it would loosen and free them.

Haller disposed of that when he and Don's uncle went over the way the currents would rise around the *Triton*. None of the hot liquid would come near the rocks; it would boil upward, doing nothing to help them.

Don finally made the inevitable suggestion which they must all have thought of. "Someone has to go outside in the bathysuit again," he said. "If the welder won't free the stuff under the rocks, maybe we can set up some kind of deflector that will throw the hot jets back where they will warm it up."

Dexter made one of his few comments. "And what will these men in the bubbles be doing then, young man?"

"Who knows?" Don admitted. "But with the welder, it shouldn't be too hard to keep them off. That's quite a weapon, if we want to use it."

"See if you can switch the viewing panel down here, will you?" Haller asked Don.

It wasn't too hard to connect one of the pickups to the small viewing screen in the wardroom. Don came back a minute later, to see a group of the bubble men standing around, performing a series of elaborate ritual gestures with their hands. It must be a code for carrying on a conversation down here, where sounds were so distorted that normal speech was impossible. And from the number and speed of their gestures; it looked as if they'd had a lot of practice.

Haller had decided the same. "That's a regular language," he commented. "I don't like it. I don't think a group could work up any set of gestures like that in even ten years."

"Maybe they live down here," Upjohn said, grinning. "There used to be a book—by a man named Charles Forte—that claimed Earth was being visited by people from Venus who lived in the sea. He thought Venus was a watery world, then."

"Why not make them Atlanteans while your imagination is working at it?" Haller asked. "All the same, somebody has been down here and has developed ways of living here for a lot longer time then I'd have thought. I'd like to know what nation has gotten the jump on us, because I don't see how any country could have been that much ahead without our scientists catching some hint. In our own waters, too!"

Don brought the conversation back to the main topic. "But what about going out in the bathysuit? They couldn't do much against that."

"They could capture it. But you may be right, Don. I've been thinking it over." It was obvious that Haller had, before Don mentioned it, for that matter. "I don't like the idea, but maybe we'll have to try. And that means asking for a volunteer. No, wait a minute."

He shook his head as Don started to offer himself again. Don had taken it for granted that he would be the one, since he was best suited to work in the device and now had the most experience. But Haller's face was grim as he held up his hand.

"It may be a suicide mission. We don't know what those men out there can do. And even if they don't try anything, they're going to get the idea at once. They'll at least bring up that supply bubble of theirs with more rocks. The only hope we have is to take off as soon as the *Triton* is free—and before they can get their supplies overhead. Maybe there'll be time enough after we're free to pick up the man in the bathysuit. Maybe not. But if I had to, I'd leave him behind and surface as fast as we could rise. This ship is more important to our country than any one of us!"

Don thought it over, and wished he could honestly volunteer. It must be a great thing to be so brave that a man could be happy in offering to die for his friends, without getting cold chills at the idea. He wiped his palms on the legs of his trousers, and tried to tell himself he wasn't really afraid. But he knew he was.

Haller looked at him, and there was warmth and sympathy in the skipper's eyes. But his voice was flat. "I can't ask anyone to go. But you're right, Don, you're the best man for the job. You *might* make it back in time. At least, you'd have a better chance than anyone else in that suit. There's nothing cowardly about turning down the job, and nobody here will think less of you if you do. Only a fool or an egomaniac wants to do a thing like that, with the risks involved. But—if you volunteer, I'll accept!"

Don't uncle cut in hotly, protesting. But Don had made up his mind, somehow. He didn't know why he was doing it, exactly, or how he managed to get his tongue unstuck from the roof of his mouth. But he nodded slowly. "Thank you, sir. I—I do volunteer."

Haller nodded gravely. "I expected it, Don. Thank

you. I'll hold the *Triton* on the bottom every second I can."

Then the fear left Don, to be replaced by a sort of numbness that was oddly mixed with satisfaction. There was a sickness down in his deepest being, but also a strange gladness that he had offered himself. He was grateful when Haller cut off the words of the others, and got down to business. If anyone had told him how brave he was, Don knew he'd have broken completely. He wasn't brave, exactly. He was only doing what the inner part of his mind told him to do.

They moved down reluctantly toward the bathysuit hatch. His uncle's face was gray and Drake looked almost as miserable. Upjohn was trying to act normal, but he was biting his lip. Don realized it was actually harder on them to see him leave than it was on him. Haller saluted him precisely and went up to the control room, with Kayne and Cavanaugh, to be ready at any moment for whatever had to be done. After a brief hesitation, Upjohn went with them, probably to take over the sonar room.

This time, getting into the bathysuit seemed to take longer. But at last, Don was settled. He nodded for them to screw down the seal on the dome of the suit, and tried not to look at his uncle's misery. Then there was quiet while they sealed the inner seal of the hatch. Don sat waiting, trying to plan his moves to bring himself nearest the hatch as he freed the last rock.

The seconds ticked by, and he still waited. Then, just as he was about to shout over the phone, he saw the inner seal open again. Drake and his uncle began unscrewing the top of the bathysuit.

It was Drake who explained, when the cover was off. "No dice, Don. The outer seal is stuck. They must have cemented it shut with that tar of theirs. We're locked in!"

Don had been struggling up. Now he dropped back helplessly, just as Haller and Upjohn came into the tool room. He could feel the reaction from his keyed-up state hit like a hot hammer smashing against soft butter.

He seemed to swell up and spatter against the walls. For a minute, his senses reeled, and the little globe swam around in front of his eyes.

Drake and Simpson were lifting him out. At a motion from Haller, they put him on one of the work tables. "Take it easy, Don," Haller said quietly. "I know what you feel like. I had something like it happen once. And don't fool yourself. You did just as much for us as if you'd freed us and died doing it. There's nothing ridiculous about it. I'm glad that hatch was sealed—and so are the rest of us."

The feeling passed finally. Don got up, still a little shaky, but able to walk without showing it. He didn't try to grin, because he knew it would be a failure. Instead, he nodded, and followed Haller back toward the control room. As he passed his uncle, Simpson put a hand on his arm; it almost unnerved him again, but it felt good.

In the sonar room, the viewing screen showed the bubble men still clustered around, but now they seemed more excited. One of them swam off and came back a minute later, pointing behind him.

Then Don saw the things for which they were waiting. Upjohn and Haller were staring at the same screen, and he heard their breaths catch.

Swimming through the water, behind a smaller group of the bubble men, were ten huge creatures of unbelievable ugliness. They looked like a cross between a crocodile and an unusually ugly fish. Their huge heads were almost all mouth and teeth, and their bodies were covered with ugly grayish warts that glowed with a faint phosphorescence. They were over twenty feet long, dwarfing the men who led them on halters of some sort.

"Ichthyosaurs," Upjohn said in surprise. "Fish lizards. The dinosaurs that took to the sea and were supposed to be extinct almost a hundred million years ago. Not like any I've seen pictured, but not too different, either."

Don saw the resemblance then. And he knew that the sea was always bringing up forms of life that were supposed to be extinct. Instead of dying out, some of the ichthyosaurs had apparently gone further and further down into the depths of the ocean, and had lasted long after all the other great reptiles had died.

"I thought they breathed air, though," he protested.

Sid nodded. "Yeah. They were supposed to, like any reptile. But you're seeing something that nobody ever saw before—an animal that not only went back to the sea, but learned to breathe water again. In maybe a hundred million years, I guess anything can happen. Look, see there by their ribs—see how the water swirls out. They don't have gills, but they've developed lungs that can handle water, and an opening below their ribs to exhaust it. Man, what a good zoologist would give for a chance to examine that lung tissue!"

Now the last of the creatures had been driven up beside the *Triton*, and Don could see that the beasts wore harnesses. More ropes were being wrapped around the *Triton*. The bubble men began hitching their beasts to the ropes, using an odd, glittering object to make the connection between the harness and the ropes. The ichthyosaurs seemed impatient to be off.

They started at a gesture from one of the bubble men. There was one of the men on the back of each beast. The lizards stretched out great flippers and began churning the water. The *Triton* stirred, and began to slide along the ooze of the bottom.

They reached the edge of the abyss finally, and the ichthyosaurs headed downward, dragging the *Triton* behind toward the depths so far below—and toward unthinkable pressures that might crack the stout walls of the ship like a walnut in a nutcracker!

CHAPTER 10/

The Bubble City

HALLER SNAPPED UP from his study. "Full speed astern!" he ordered sharply. The downward movement had been smooth and effortless before. But as the great jets lashed out, there was a feeling of wrenching inside the ship. On the screen, the bow pickup showed the sea men and their mounts scattering wildly to the side. But their ropes were long enough, apparently, to permit them to move off to the side out of the wash of the jets and still keep dragging the ship down. The jets slowed the *Triton's* descent, but could not stop it.

A big bubble flashed up from below at an amazing speed, and came to a stop beside the ship. There were men inside it. Apparently it could be enlarged or contracted to vary the displacement of water, and hence make it rise or sink as they wanted. Now it hovered, while other man in bubbles moved into it. Don could see no sign of doors, but the men moved in effortlessly, as if the walls weren't there. For that matter, there was no sign of anything that could be called a wall. The water just seemed to end and the air to begin.

A bulky piece of apparatus was being assembled inside the bubble, apparently from a group of smaller units. Each part looked like a four-inch crystal cube, with a black box under it. It was similar to one of the things worn on the back of the men. The final equipment was simply a group of such things attached together.

The bubble floated over beside the *Triton*, nearly touching. A smaller bubble was shoved out, with the equipment inside. Then that bubble suddenly disappeared, and the apparatus drifted against the wall of the *Triton* and stuck there. Don could see only a portion of it at the far edge of one of the pickup's angle of view.

One of the bubble men suddenly darted ahead of the ship, just beyond the reach of the jets, and began making frantic gestures toward the hot steam and water issuing from the ship.

"Threatening us?" Upjohn asked.

Haller shook his head doubtfully. "Doesn't look like it—but I can't be sure. Kayne, get on the jet control. Be ready to cut at my signal. It looks as if he's warning us of something. . . ."

Abruptly, the *Triton* was surrounded by a bubble that lay about half an inch beyond its hull. It looked as if it had started out touching the hull and been pushed beyond almost at once.

"Cut jets!" Haller shouted. The navigator threw the lever and the meters flopped over. With the bubble around them, the jets could get no water to cool the atomic reactor, and had to be cut before they could overheat.

But that left them completely helpless. Shep had been curled up sleeping through most of the excitement. Now he got up, sniffing doubtfully. He smelled around the control room, casting unhappy looks at Don. Then he lifted his nose and let out a wild, low howl. Don reached for him, and ordered him to be quiet. Shep sank back then, without another sound, but with a worried, uncertain expression.

"Something about the way that bubble is made that he doesn't like," Haller said. "Maybe something like a static charge that we can't sense. And maybe he reacts some to our emotions."

They were still going down. Don tried to guess their rate of descent and add the amount they had dropped to their original depth. It came out to a figure that he hated to consider. They would soon be close to two thousand fathoms down—over two miles, and where the pressure would exceed the two tons per square inch that was all the *Triton* had been built to stand for even short times.

He looked at the pressure gauge, and frowned. It was registering less than twenty-five hundred pounds and going down rapidly. Either whatever was making the bubble had interfered with its operation or else it had been broken in one of the series of shocks.

He wondered for a second if they could have turned around and be moving upward. But the pressure of his feet on the deck told him unmistakably that there was a definite down direction, and that they were heading that way.

"How deep is it here?" Haller asked him.

He tried to remember, but couldn't be sure of the figure directly below the edge of the cliff; he couldn't know definitely whether they were heading straight down or drifting horizontally, either.

"From the minimum of about seven thousand to a maximum of over twenty thousand feet—about twenty-five thousand in some places," he answered. "And we weren't too near any minimum spots, except for that one plateau."

"So we could drop to four thousand fathoms," Haller said. "That's better than five tons to the inch. Hmm. We *would* be over the Milwaukee Deep when it happened."

The bubble around them seemed to have lightened them until the *Triton* now weighed practically the same as the water they displaced. The ship was moving smoothly, being drawn down by the ichthyosaurs. Don studied the scene on the panel, and blinked as he saw a new detail he must have overlooked before. The bubble ran out along the towropes, keeping its distance from the cords the same as its distance from the hull. But where the odd plastic or crystal hitches joined the rope to the harness of the ichthyosaurs, the bubble ended abruptly, closing in just before it could touch the hitches.

When Don pointed this out, Simpson studied it, and traced the bubble back and forth from ship to hitch. "I don't know how they do it," he admitted. "It's new to me. They must have some science that we haven't hit yet. It acts like a controlled electrostatic shield—though I don't know exactly what that would be, either."

Drake could give no better explanation. "Unless you figure on these tractor and pressor rays the men on those space-opera programs throw around. If the pressor ray were anything more than just a meaningless word—and if you could make one lie down on its side and hug the ship—it might act like that. Something's keeping the water away from the hull. Maybe they've learned what the energy that binds the atom together is. Call it binding force energy—one form of it—for want of a better name. But it's only a name—it doesn't explain anything."

"It only muddies the water," Simpson protested. "You men who talk about exact science are always pulling a razzle-dazzle with words. If you'd learn a little engineering . . ."

Then he stopped, realizing that this wasn't the time and place for his favorite argument over whether theoretical science or applied engineering was more valuable to human progress.

Upjohn filled the gap in the conversation. "As long as we're all going to go down to our death with a fine, philosophical conversation, you might consider those ichthyosaurs again. Men don't domesticate animals unless they live around them. If we came down here with all the science those boys out there have, we'd never think of taming those beasts. We'd use machinery. But if we grew up down here, with the lizards around all the time, some of us would decide to use them."

"You mean those people live down here?" Haller asked.

"I don't know. But it looks like it. The clothes they wear might be a disguise—but they don't act as if they were wearing anything but normal clothes. The science doesn't fit ours. And they don't even look like people we usually see. They remind me of some figures I've seen in museums. Cro-Magnards—the men from the Cro-Magnon."

Don blinked, and stared out again. But now that he thought of it, Upjohn was right. They did look a little like the reconstructions he had seen and studied. Cro-Magnon man had replaced Neanderthal man in Europe somewhere between fifty and twenty-five thousand years before, and had then either disappeared or been absorbed by other races. He'd left his bones, and the beautiful colored pictures of his life on the walls of his caves. With his large brain and fine physical structure, he seemed almost superior to the races that had survived.

"Nonsense," Drake said. "No race could live down here. Those men don't breathe water like the lizards. Maybe they could adapt to the pressure in enough centuries. But they couldn't maintain life down here without a lot of science, and primitive men never had that."

"What about Atlantis?" Upjohn asked, grinning at Haller. "We have accounts there of a scientific race long before our time."

Haller grunted this time. "A bunch of mythology. The Greeks claimed they had heard about it from Egyptian priests, who never told where they heard it. And ever since, people have been taking what was meant to be a good story seriously. There are a lot of myths about continents that sink into the ocean, but no scientific evidence has been found. No, this wouldn't have anything to do with either Plato's Greek Atlantis or some of the later nonsense men have used to explain things that already had a better explanation. And you know it, Sid."

"Sure," Sid Upjohn admitted. "I know it. But do they? Anyhow, I wasn't too serious about Atlantis. But you might consider the number of stories about mermaids and mermen. Because out there, unless I'm crazy, is a race of people who have lived here long enough to domesticate animals."

Dexter smiled faintly, and nodded. "If you'd look at your screen, I'm afraid you'd have to agree with Mr. Upjohn."

They turned quickly to stare where he pointed. There were more people out there now—and a different crowd. Among the men were others dressed in fuller costumes, extending from neck to near the knee, with a split skirt something like a pair of jodhpurs, something like a woman's bicycle skirt. They were obviously women, now staring at the ship the men were dragging home. And with them were even a few smaller figures that must have been children. All were in the bubbles, and the crowd of bubble people was growing steadily.

"All right," Haller admitted. "You win, Sid. When you find women and children around, I guess it means they live here. We're collecting quite a crowd."

The gathering grew by the second. Don studied these people. Except for the pallor of their skins and their odd costumes, they were rather attractive. They must have averaged over six feet in height, with straight figures. Their heads were a trifle large, but the sharp planes of their faces hid this. He saw no one who was either too fat or too thin; in fact, they seemed surprisingly alike, even to their faintly golden hair.

Haller sighed, and swung back from the screen. "All of which is fine—but it doesn't get us out of this. We can be crushed just as flat being captured by genuine sea people as by some enemy nation down here. How deep are we?"

Kayne stared morosely at the useless depth gauge, which now registered a depth of about three feet on its fine dial. "I estimate we must be down to about three miles—a little over three tons per square inch. But it may be nearer four."

They were still going down. Don sat frozen, staring at the useless gauge, trying to make the figures mean something. Over fifteen thousand feet down, with a pressure of more than six thousand pounds on every square inch. That meant nearly a million pounds for every square foot. He'd taken the ability of the *Triton's* hull to stand such pressures for granted before, but now it seemed impossible that anything under any conditions could endure.

Yet there was still life swimming in the water. Every so often, a strange thing would flash by, or pass near the people. One looked like an old oak root that had been dug up and had sprouted new twigs with leaves. It swam along by moving its "roots" in a totally fantastic way. One of the young girls outside reached out and shoved her hand down into it, to come up with a tiny thing that looked like it, except for size. The bigger one stopped swimming and began to curl up until she put the little one back among the twisting arms. Nothing like that had been in any of the pictures Don had seen.

Brought to the surface, such a form would explode with all the violence of a bomb. The pressures inside, now equalized by the outside water pressure, were simply impossible to picture.

They were still going down, but more slowly now. Ahead, the ichthyosaurs had stretched out in a fan-like arrangement and were paddling along. Don went to the sonar gear, but could get no response. The bubble cut it off completely. He had no way of finding how much further down the bottom lay.

Abruptly, they leveled off completely, so far as he could tell. Now the lizards seemed to pick up speed, as if heading for some place they knew.

The crowd began to stream away. Some of them swam along casually, drifting behind. But most had either the small sleds with propellers or else held something that looked like a brief case, also with a propeller sticking out from it. These began leaving the ship behind, as they disappeared into murkiness beyond which the ship's lights could not penetrate.

Cavanaugh had been standing by the helm all during the trip. Now Haller looked up, and seemed to become suddenly aware of this. He motioned toward the galley. "Better knock off, Paul, and get something. No sense in your standing by the helm now."

The big man threw a glance back that was a mixture

of worry and amusement. "Ever see a car towed on a line, sir? It needs someone at the wheel. Same here. We ride a lot smoother when I keep the ship centered behind them."

"You mean the rudder still works?" Simpson asked sharply. Then he nodded to himself. "Yes, it would. If the bubble around us is that thin, it wouldn't make much difference in steering."

"Take over, Kayne," Haller suggested. "Thanks, Paul."

The navigator took the controls, but Cavanaugh remained beside him, staring into the screen he had been using to guide the ship behind the ichthyosaurs. "Something up ahead," he reported.

Don had been using a side pickup to study the crowd. Now he switched to the forward one. Cavanaugh was right. There seemed to be a faint glow of light ahead that was increasing rapidly as they cut through the dark water.

Slowly, they made out the outlines of a great bubble, about a mile in diameter, and perhaps five hundred feet high, like a bowl of glass turned upside down. It glowed in the surrounding gloom, but there were outlines of buildings inside. As they drew closer the city took on more details. It conformed to the outlines of the dome, except that no building rose for more than seven or eight stories in height. White and black stone seemed to be the basic building materials, and the architecture varied from almost Grecian simplicity in the center to things that looked like rough adobe houses near the edge.

Upjohn chuckled. "Welcome to Atlantis, gentlemen. And don't tell the inhabitants that it doesn't exist, or that they're just myths. They might not like it."

CHAPTER 11 /

Atlantis

THEY WERE BEING PULLED toward a section of the dome which was not crowded with buildings. Beyond it, and touching the dome on the inside, was a pool of water, perhaps fifty feet longer than the *Triton,* and three times her width. There were half a dozen children swimming about in it—with no bubbles surrounding them now—who were being chased out as the *Triton* was drawn up.

The ichthyosaurs drew as close to the bubble as they could, and then stopped. Some of the men uncoupled them and led them off, while others seized the ropes that had been towing the ship. They headed for the dome confidently, and moved through it with no sign of effort. As they stepped through, the *Triton* began to move after them. The bottom of the pool was about fifteen feet higher than the floor of the ocean here— apparently most of the city was above sea level, and only held in place by the bubble around it.

There was no feeling as the *Triton* touched the bubble. They began sliding through without any resistance. Simpson whistled.

"No resistance at all," he said. "They walk through it as if it were air—and yet it holds back the ocean on one side, and is supporting that wrecked house on the other."

One of the men towing the *Triton* suddenly jerked to a halt, half falling over. The others gave every indication of laughing as he swung around and came back through the bubble. The hitch which had connected the ichthyosaur harness with the towrope had not been removed, and it was this, striking the bubble, which had snapped him back. Obviously, the plastic or crystal was an insulator of some kind against the spreading of the bubble, and it couldn't pass through.

Drake rubbed his hands over his hair, and stared as the man went through easily, after removing the hitch. "A field of force of some kind," he decided. "It has to be. It isn't there, in the sense that normal matter is. It's just a line drawn that says so far and no further. Like the so-called magnetic lines around a magnet—except here all the lines are together in the shape they want it to take. But there *isn't* any such field. Maybe I was right. Maybe it's nuclear-binding energy—in this case, the same energy that keeps the electron from rushing straight to the proton."

"How do the men get through?" Haller asked. "And the ship?"

"Because they're enclosed in the same stuff. Notice, when they're almost through, they turn off the stuff, and it melts into the main field. It seems one field can penetrate another—but nothing that isn't in a shield can get through. Heck, I don't know. According to the science I learned, that couldn't exist. But it does, so we have to accept it. For all I know, it has absolutely infinite strength."

The *Triton* was almost through now, gliding into the former swimming pool. It was a little bumpy, since the bubble men had apparently had to guess how its weight was distributed, and hadn't always been right. But eventually, the *Triton* was inside.

Abruptly, the bubble around them cut off.

Kayne reached for the jet control. "Maybe we can blast out, while they're not expecting it—" he began.

Haller pushed his hand from the control. "No! That wall, or whatever it is, wouldn't let us through, now that the bubble's gone. And if you start running the jets in here, you'll contaminate their water and spray it all over. We can't poison them with radioactives yet."

"Why not, sir? They attacked us."

"Maybe they figure it the other way around. Maybe they've got a boundary line up there. Everything above it belongs to our people, everything below to theirs. When we crossed the border, they went into action, of course. We can't figure they're any less human than we are, just because they happen to live differently. They're not the same—but that doesn't mean they're any better or worse."

Kayne stared at him with a touch of sullenness. "They're enemies of our country. They've committed an act of piracy."

"Nonsense. They haven't hurt us. They probably never meant us to come to any harm. They're simply picking up people who are trespassing. This is *their* territory, Kayne."

Simpson sighed in the back of the group. "I'm not sure about their not hurting us. We've stood the pressure so far, somehow—I allowed a safety factor in building the hull, but this is more than I had in mind. We can't take it forever."

"Probably they don't realize the pressure is dangerous to us. Why come down here, if it is, from their point of view. Maybe they think we've let the pressure inside the ship go up to as high as it is outside."

"Air that much compressed would burn out our lungs—we couldn't stand so much oxygen," Don suggested. He'd been trying to figure it out. With four hundred times normal pressure or more, a man breathing such air should be able to hold his breath for over six hours! But of course, nobody could breathe it at all. Oxygen is a corrosive gas, which is why it unites with so many things and gives off heat in fires. The lungs were meant to make use of it—but not when four hundred times as much was acting all at once. He wondered how the city outside could exist.

Drake answered it for him before he could ask. "They must have an atmosphere that's mostly some inert gas—nitrogen, helium, or some such. Probably not much more oxygen in it than in our own air."

"They seem to want to test it on us," Cavanaugh said. In the screen, one of the men was making motions which could only mean that he wanted them to come out. He was older then most of the others, with grayer skin and snow-white hair. He was also set apart by a beard, which was worn by no one else they had seen, and by a sort of robe that came down to below his knees.

"Hospitable city, Atlantis," Upjohn remarked. "He wants us to come out and be squashed flat."

"You insist on calling it Atlantis," Haller said. Don was beginning to wonder how much of the conversation was meant, and how much of it was just an effort to cover up the nerves and worry. "Why not call it Lemuria? That was another country that sank beneath the ocean, according to the legends."

Upjohn shook his head sternly. "No. Never. That was supposed to be in the Pacific. Anyhow, why not Atlantis? This is in the Atlantic Ocean. People in America are Americans—people in the Atlantic are Atlanteans—which is what the citizens of Atlantis are called."

Outside, the old man was making more insistent gestures, and a couple of others in robes had appeared. Finally, he shrugged and seemed to give up. He made a quick motion toward the ship with his hand.

A group of other men dressed in dark blue came forward, pushing a cart loaded with various tools and equipment. They headed straight for the bathysuit hatch, where some of their people had seen Don come and go.

Haller frowned as they began choosing tools. "They're more than hospitable. They're too insistent. Dr. Simpson, can they find a way to open the hatch?"

"I don't see how," Don's uncle answered. "It locks on the inside, and is about as tough a job as any safe-cracker might have. They may be able to get into the hatch. The outer seal has a manual lever, and if they work it right, they'll have no trouble. But we've got the inner seal secured."

The Atlanteans had no trouble at all with the outer seal. In less than five minutes, they were dragging out the cumbersome bathysuit. Then they disappeared with their tools into the hatch.

Haller switched the screen over to the wardroom and started back, with the others following. Senator Kenney was standing there, drawing a cup of coffee, his eyes red from sleep. He looked almost cheerful for him.

"Good work, Admiral," he greeted Haller. "I felt sure you'd get us away from those aliens in the bubbles. I noticed how calm everything was when I awoke, so I knew we'd surfaced safely. When do we start back for the base?"

Haller pointed to the screen that showed the crowd outside and those near the bathysuit hatch. A fair amount of the city spread out beyond it. Kenney studied it, smiling at first. Then he seemed less certain.

"I'm afraid I don't place this base. And you've got some odd workmen repairing the ship. Secret government base, I suppose. Or can you tell me where we are?"

"Approximately three miles below the surface, somewhere in the Milwaukee Deep," Haller told him. "Those people are the bubble men, and this is their city, which Sid here calls Atlantis. Right now, they're trying to break into the ship. If they do, the pressure in the ocean at this depth is measured in tons per inch. If they don't . . . Well, we'll think about that later."

Kenney stared at Haller, putting his coffee down slowly. "You mean, Admiral, that you let this ship be captured? You let them take us, knowing I was aboard—and with the McCurdy bill coming up next week on the floor of the Senate! You mean you're just sitting here, while they try to break in. Admiral Haller,

I wonder if you realize that the matter of naval appropriations . . . But you're joking, of course."

He started to pick up the cup again, and his eyes rested on the screen. He set the coffee back. "You *are* joking, aren't you? We—we're safe?"

"We're probably less safe than any other thirteen men alive, Senator," Haller said.

Kenney stared in fascination at him and back to the screen. He shook his head very slowly. "You're not joking. No. Admiral, I'm an old man! I've got to get back to Washington. They want to put through that bill— raise the tax on tobacco. My state can't stand another such raise, sir. I promised to fight it, and I intend to fight it. I . . . No, you're not joking. I—I don't quite know what to say."

He lifted the coffee and drank it carefully, never pulling the cup away from his mouth until it was empty. He set it down, wiped his lips slowly, and nodded. "Very good. Excellent. . . . Admiral Haller, I consider your conduct in this affair an appalling example of egregious incompetence, and I intend to see that something is done about it. Gross and egregious incompetence! I won't *stand* for it. I've had enough! Sir, I'll give you exactly 'one hour—exactly—to return this ship to the surface. Not another minute. Those foreign spies out there don't fool me with their fake sets. And neither do you, you traitor to your country. Yes, sir, traitor! A man who would steal this ship and deliberately turn it over to an alien power is the lowest, vilest, sorriest scum that ever infested this fair . . . How far down?"

"Three miles. And we're locked in down here."

"I'm getting old," Kenney said. "I'm ten years older than my constituents think. Seventy-nine this summer. Sometimes I think I can't remember things well. Forty years in the Senate, and now they won't re-elect me again. But I guess I'm just an old bag of wind, at that. Bad temper, silly, out of touch with reality. Forgive me—I'm upset. There's no chance to escape, I take it? No. No, so I gather. I guess it's a good thing they sent me instead of some of the younger men. There are some excellent men in the Senate, Admiral. Not like me—like I was thirty years ago, rather, when I was a good man. They can get along without me. Nobody'll miss me. Well, I've done some good work in my time. Now I'm just a hanger-on, all bad temper because I know I'm not much of a man. Thank you for your courtesy, sir. I won't trouble you further."

He went to the opposite side of the wardroom and sank onto a seat. From one pocket, he produced a handkerchief and began wiping his glasses slowly and carefully.

Don turned away uncomfortably. It wasn't nice to see a man who knew he didn't count any more, and who was driven by fear and bad luck to the point where he found it necessary to admit it. Kenney had been a good man once, according to his record. But he'd been through a long siege of sickness years before, and had never quite regained his abilities. Probably the newspaper stories of his temper hadn't helped.

There was a sick silence for a few minutes. Then they went back to watching the screen. But there was nothing there to see. The pickup couldn't look around a corner to see how the Atlanteans were doing in the hatch.

Suddenly the screen leaped with splashes of zig-zag color as static cut through the image. But that was ridiculous, Don knew. This signal was carried over shielded wire, and not picked up like normal television. It should be completely free from static. Yet the crackle and hiss of wild energy somewhere near went on.

Then there was a clang from below. Haller cut off the screen sharply and swung about to face toward the bow. From below came the sounds of feet moving across a metal deck, and up the little stairs.

"They couldn't—" Simpson began. But Drake cut him off.

"They did. If they can use binding energy—it has to be that—of one kind, maybe they can use other kinds. And some of those energies hold the atoms together. Do something to that force, and they could push the door down with their hands, for all we know. Anyhow, they're in."

The feet drew nearer, and with it came a whiff of strange air, carrying the odd odor of the sea. But the pressure hadn't crushed them inside! Don struggled with that idea, as the others must be doing. He tried to remember whether the outer seal had been closed again. Then he knew that it had remained open.

The air inside the bubble was at almost the same pressure as the air on the surface! That meant that the thin bubble of whatever it was could stand the incredible pressure of the sea. The *Triton* had been protected by the bubble around her, or they might already have been squashed by that incredible force.

Then the steps were in front of them, and he looked up to see six men standing there with some odd instrument that might be a weapon in the hands of one. The Atlantean motioned them forward.

Haller stood up slowly. But Kenney came to his feet first. He leaped from his seat and almost ran toward the Atlantean.

"Traitor! Spy!" he screamed. "You'll never get this ship. You shan't have it, I tell you. Your whole city can go hang! You—you *monster!* You alien, sneaking, spying monster!"

His thin old fist came up from his waist to strike squarely into the Atlantean's face.

The man drew back, blinking. Then his lips twisted suddenly, and the weapon leaped up in his hands, with a crackling sound coming from it. He swung it slowly toward the crew of the *Triton*.

Shep let out a snarling growl and charged. In mid-leap, he fell to the deck and went skidding across it, limp and unconscious. Don saw his friends begin to fall, and then it hit him. A violent electric shock seemed to leap through him, and his mind blacked out.

CHAPTER 12 /

City of No Return

DON CAME TO with a vague memory of men standing around him and of a sharp pain in his arm. But the room in which he found himself was deserted.

Light came down softly from a ceiling that seemed to glow all over with a soft fluorescence. He looked around, to find himself in a place perhaps ten feet square, with bare stone walls and a plastic floor. There were no windows, and only a single door, now tightly closed. The room was bare of furniture, except for the hard pad on which he lay, raised about a foot from the floor, and a padded stool across the room.

His arm itched, and he glanced down to see that his sleeve had been rolled up. Near his elbow, a spot of bright red indicated that his memory of the pain must have been correct; something had been injected while he was unconscious.

He got up, surprised to find no sickness or headache, and went to the door. There were two levers at about the height of a doorknob. If they were supposed to be squeezed together, then they must be locked now, since they could not be moved. He was locked in!

"Hey!" He yelled, and then yelled again as he got no answer. He kicked at the door, but it seemed to be made of heavy stone, and gave off only a faint, muffled sound. If the rest of the crew were in nearby rooms, they couldn't hear him.

He was just dropping onto the pad again when the door opened quickly and an old man stepped in, to close it sharply behind him. It was the same man Don had seen outside the ship inside the city. At closer view, his white hair and beard were somewhat disordered, and his robe was of a coarse material. He set a bowl of something that looked like rice pudding and a metal goblet of water before Don.

The boy realized he was thirsty, and swallowed the water quickly. But the fishy-tasting food didn't appeal to him. He pushed it away and regarded the old man. Then he saw the weapon in the other's hand and gave up any wild notions.

"Okay," he said. "So I'll be good. What do we do now. Point to things and start learning the language? I'm Don."

He indicated himself, and repeated the word. Maybe if he could get the other started on teaching him and wait until the old man was off guard, he could somehow get the weapon. . . .

"I'm Muggins," the old man said, and his lips parted in a wide grin. His English was as good as Don's except for a faint New England twang. "And we wait here until K'mith is ready to see you."

Don's mouth dropped open. He should have been used to surprises. Screens that kept back the weight of the ocean, cities under the sea, gadgets that could break down steel doors—and now English!

"Don't be so dratted surprised," the old man told him, and his grin broadened. "No reason I shouldn't speak English. I was born in Gloucester."

"You mean—you're all from the United States?"

Muggins shook his head. "Only me. The others came from right here. Been here since I donno when. I've been here more than fifty years myself. Came down in a submarine that got hit in the war. German sub torpedoed us, and down we went. Pressure broke us open, and water started squirting in. I got to the escape hatch.

Knew it wouldn't do any good, but had to try something. No sooner out, then something slaps me in the back and one of them bubbles springs up all around me. K'mayo—that'd be K'mith's older brother that died years ago. . . . He'd been watching, hoping somebody'd come out. He wanted to find out about the world up above, and he needed someone who'd teach him the language. So he brought me back to Mlayanu here—and here I still am."

"Then you'll help us?" Don was up from the cot, new hope running through him. "You've got a weapon, and maybe you know where all the others are. Help us get away, and we'll take you back with us in the *Triton!* They won't expect . . ."

Muggins shook his head again and the grin vanished. "Nope. No reason I should try to get away. They saved my life, and they treated me all right here. I like it. Got a wife, family, friends. I don't mind if you can escape— but don't count on my helping you. This here's my city, and I ain't turning traitor to it. Anyhow, you couldn't get out. You've got a blamed sight better ship than we ever had, but it ain't that good. When you get in here, there's no going back. And don't figure you can swipe a suit and go up to the surface. That stuff goes fine in the books, but here the bubble-suits aren't allowed for anyone without a permit—and his family, if he says so. Once you get to Mlayanu, there's no return to the surface. Sooner you learn that, the better off you'll be."

"What about the others?" Don asked. He could see by Muggins' expression that it would do no good to argue. And it was hardly worth making plans for escape when all he'd seen of the interior of the city was a single room!

Muggins relaxed, and his smile came back. "Reckon I can show you that. Don't get me wrong, youngster. I'll do anything I can for you people—I'm tickled pink to see somebody from the surface. Use to dream about getting a chance to pay a visit up there again." He went to the wall and shoved back a small flush-set panel Don hadn't noticed, revealing a glass-covered opening.

"Your friends are in there. Been before the Council all morning. I guess they're waiting to hear the results."

Don looked, and his heart sank. All twelve of the men from the *Triton* were there, but he could tell from their expressions that things had gone anything but well. He spotted his uncle talking unhappily with Drake and Haller. Then he frowned. In the back of the room, and held by four strong chains, was Shep.

The dog was chewing futilely at the metal. Now he seemed to see Don, and tried to stand up, opening his mouth in what looked like a bark, though no sound came through. At the same time, Simpson glanced toward the window. Don's uncle got up quickly and came to the glass, making motions.

Muggins closed the panel at once, and Don went back to the pad. "What will happen to them?" he asked. "And why am I separate?"

"Dunno what," Muggins answered. "No precedent for this. I don't reckon they'll hurt your friends much. You? Heck, here you're just a baby. They figure you're a child. Mlayanu kids don't even start school till they're eighteen. Before that, they're not supposed to know or amount to much."

There was a muffled sound from the door, and the old man went to it. He stuck his head out, and a babble of liquid-sounding conversation began. At last, the old man nodded, and turned back to Don.

"Come along. K'mith wants to see you now."

Don got up and followed the older man. Whoever had spoken before was gone, and there was nothing but a long hallway, lighted by the same glowing ceiling as had been in his room. They went past doors and up a ramp, to follow a somewhat better hallway; the layout was the same, but the stone was better-grained and the doors now had peculiar curlicues on them.

Muggins finally stopped at one of the doors. He tapped on it, and waited. There was a faint sound from inside. The old man opened the door and motioned Don inside.

The room was somewhat fancier. There was a mat on

the floor, and benches along the walls. In the center of the room, a large man about fifty-five sat at a boxlike desk. His complexion was gray and his hair the yellow-white of all the Atlanteans, but his face seemed squarer than any other Don had seen.

"K'mith," Muggins introduced him. "And it's an honor down here to have only that much of a name. So call him that. He wants to ask you some questions."

Don nodded, studying the man. He seemed to be a man of considerable strength, but his face was pleasant, and a rugged smile somehow gave the feeling of natural warmth. K'mith's arm moved, indicating a small seat by the desk, and Don dropped onto it.

"You might tip me off if I say something wrong," he suggested to Muggins.

The big head of K'mith tilted back, and a low laugh came from his mouth. He sobered quickly, however. "That was the first wrong something, Don Miller," he said in precise English, with only a faint accent. "As you can hear, I have learned your language—from Muggins and from the books which my people have rescued from your ships that sank, before the water ruined them." He indicated a shelf of books that had obviously been water-soaked and carefully dried. "Also, we send up an antenna and sometimes listen to your radio. That is how we heard of atomic-powered submarines. Naturally, we were interested, and have been trying to discover one. Yours was the first we located in our scouting. Are there many such ships?"

Don nodded. "A lot, not counting the cargo ones," he admitted. There was no point in telling K'mith that those were all older models, not related to the *Triton*.

K'mith nodded thoughtfully in turn. "So. I heard it, but so much of your books and radio is not true— fiction you call it, though we say it lies. And of course, all your adults have been schooled to the fantasies, so I can learn nothing from them. Even Muggins here, though he is a good man."

It was obvious from Muggins' grunt that this was a

sore subject. But after reading a mixture of *Gulliver's Travels, Alice in Wonderland,* and Haggard's *She,* K'mith had reason to be confused. The books were an odd mixture of fiction and out-of-date fact books. Don saw that one was a copy of Plato's *Republic,* and wondered how that serious but impossible scheme of government compared with what K'mith had heard.

K'mith had followed Don's quick glance. He grimaced. "An odd world you have. All your books are fantasies, it seems. Truth may be in them, but I cannot find the key that tells what is true. And your friends will not help. At what age do your children start to school?"

Don started to answer. Then he saw Muggins gesturing below the table. Don stared at the figure the old man was writing. "Eighteen," he said, without thinking, reading the figure aloud.

K'mith let out a satisfied chuckle before Don could correct himself. "Aha. The same age as we use. Naturally—who would risk burning out the delicate mind of a child before it was ripe enough for study? So I can learn the truth from a child who can't know anything I need—and I get only lies from those who may know."

"I know enough," Don said quickly. "Would you let us all go back, if . . ."

K'mith shook his head, looking like a father laughing at a child. "No, Don Miller. Don't pretend things. And you needn't worry. We don't punish children for the acts of their adult friends. You'll be treated just like one of our own children. Muggins will find you a place to stay until you're a few months older. Then we'll find a teacher for you. In a few years, you'll be one of us. For now, go out and meet some other children and enjoy yourself. You're quite free, as long as you don't try to leave the city."

"What about the others?" Don asked.

K'mith shrugged. "That's a problem between adults, Don Miller," he said, and held out his hand. "Thank you for seeing me. When you are eighteen, I'll help you pick a teacher. Now good-by."

Don tried to protest, but Muggins was beside him, steering him out. They began threading their way down the hall again, before Don could face the old man. "What was the idea of making me say eighteen?"

"Pretty simple, youngster. Now they think you're uneducated, so you're harmless. You can do just about anything you like. Otherwise, you'd have been locked up, or something. It made a liar out of me, but I figured it'd help you. Do don't go kicking about favors done you."

Don turned it over. It would have advantages, at that. He'd had thirteen years of schooling, with added study given by his uncle, but people would think he knew nothing. Definitely, it put him at an advantage. He should be able to figure some way to get the others out of that room where they were being kept.

Muggins caught him suddenly, and tried to turn him. But Don resisted, long enough to see what had caught the old man's attention. Then he gasped.

Passing down a corridor that crossed the hall he was on were the others from the *Triton*. Each wore a crude set of handcuffs with a weight attached that pulled their hands down in front of them. And they were surrounded by more than a dozen guards, each armed with the weapons he had seen used before.

His uncle was toward the rear, walking hopelessly, with his face a picture of sick misery.

"Uncle Eddy!" Don shouted.

Simpson looked up, and surprise gave place to pleasure and then to determination. He jerked his arms up, bringing the weight above his hips and suddenly broke out of the group, running toward Don. The guards let out a surprised shout, and started after Simpson. The others from the *Triton* immediately blocked their way.

Simpson was almost at the corner, where he could swing down it and perhaps dart into one of the offices. Don jumped for one at random and tried the door. It started to open, and Simpson headed for it.

Then there was a faint hissing sound, and Don's uncle collapsed in a heap. The guard who had fired his weapon came forward and lifted him up, slinging Simpson over his shoulder and heading back to the group.

Don started toward them, but Muggins' hand fell on his shoulder. "None of that, Don. You've made trouble enough. Now you come along peacefully or I'll have to stungun you."

"Go ahead," Don told him bitterly. "Go on. You expect me to stand here quietly while they take Uncle Eddy and the others off to be executed or something?"

"They won't be hurt. They're just being put where they can't make any trouble. Jail, you might say. I tell you, they don't kill people down here. They don't even mistreat people unless they have to. At least, I never heard of anyone being hurt." But Muggins sounded doubtful as he finished.

Don saw that the group had vanished beyond his sight. He let Muggins lead him outside, still burning with resentment at the treatment he had seen. "They have no right . . ."

"Maybe not," Muggins agreed. "But they can't let your people escape, youngster. They have to be locked up. Prisoners of state, I guess. They know too much to be let go. And don't go planning to go getting them out or running off yourself. I told you before—this is the city of no return. Once you get here, you stay here!"

CHAPTER 13 /

The Dog-God

"THERE'S NO PLACE THAT CAN'T BE ESCAPED," Don argued hotly. "It just takes more work and skill in some places. If you think you can keep me from trying by scaring me off, you're wrong!"

The old man chuckled. "You think so? Ever try figuring how you'd stand the pressure once you got out? Without a license, you couldn't get one of those suits. They're kept locked up good and tight. And you'd sure need a bubble to get out of here. Anyhow, once you got to the surface, how'd anyone ever find you?"

"There's the submarine," Don pointed out. "If you think I'm going to let K'mith or anyone else hold the whole crew prisoners, while he tries to blow everyone up working on the atomic plant . . ."

"Don't know anything about atomic plants," Muggins said stubbornly. "But I know this place. I should. If they got you with a whole crew aboard, how you figure you can get the machine out alone? How you gonna get it through the dome?"

Don had no idea, but he couldn't admit defeat. Not when K'mith left him free, and the others were being kept prisoners for life, or worse. They wouldn't be hurt for a while, though; the Atlanteans would need the crew, if they intended to try to learn more about atomics.

Then a familiar sound caught his ear. It was the short, protesting bark of a dog. There was no question in Don's mind. It was Shep's bark. And the last time he'd seen the dog in chains. . . .

"Shep!" he yelled.

Immediately, the barks rose to a frenzy, with a new note added. Don started toward the sound at a run, with Muggins trailing along behind. He shot around a corner, and then down the street toward the sounds. They seemed to be coming from the back of the same big building from which he had just come.

He reached a little square behind it—and spotted Shep. The dog was fastened with half a dozen small ropes, and each was held by an Atlantean. The six men stretched out to form a network that kept Shep from leaping in any direction. He was hopping up and down wildly, trying to get his mouth around to tear at the ropes, but not succeeding. When he caught sight of Don, he seemed to go crazy. One of the men reached for a stungun.

"Quiet, Shep!" Don ordered. "Down!"

The dog stopped his noise at once and settled down to the stone paving, panting furiously but obeying the familiar commands. Don swung about, studying the men who were around. Then he spotted K'mith at the top of the stone steps. The big man was coming toward him with a curious expression on his face.

"What are they doing with my dog?" Don demanded.

K'mith frowned in quick surprise. "*Your* dog, Don Miller? Then those books . . . But what do you want with him?"

"He's my pet, my friend," Don answered. "What goes on here, anyhow?"

The Atlantean studied the quiet animal thoughtfully. "Once," he said, and he sounded as if he were quoting, "men lived on the forbidden highest level, and there they were surrounded by great beasts. And the beasts were wild and savage, killing the men and destroying them. There were beasts higher than houses, and beasts smaller than the hand. But they all bit and trampled and killed. And when the upper level rested in darkness, that showed the god's displeasure that man had found only half his proper way, then the beasts came roaring and wailing out of this darkness, since some of the beasts were angry gods, who led the others. And no man could stay the strong jaw and the savage teeth."

"You may be remembering your people's accounts," Don told him. "But my people had a tough time of it, too, and they tamed the dogs to help them. Maybe that's the start of our whole civilization. Shep isn't any wild beast. He's an old friend."

K'mith considered it. Finally he indicated that the men holding the ropes should let them go. Their faces froze at that, but after a few words in the language of the city, K'mith convinced them somehow. They dropped the ropes and ran back as fast as their legs would carry them. Only K'mith remained beside the boy.

"C'mere, Shep," Don said.

Shep was up at a single leap, hopping stiff-legged into the air and trying to lick Don's face. There was a shriek from the crowd, then an awed mutter of surprise as Don stretched out his arms and Shep leaped into them. The animal wriggled and licked happily, whining faintly, until Don finally put him down. Then he began running in circles around his master.

"Wild, yes," K'mith decided. "But not dangerous. Come with me—just beyond this corner." He led the way, until they had rounded the corner of the building, and then pointed to another small square with a statue mounted on a pedestal.

The statue was probably carved from pure tradition. No animal had ever looked like it. The parts were from several animals—the head even had a bit of a trunk and tusks. But oddly enough, it was a little like Shep.

The crowd had streamed after them, and now a great cry began to go up. Muggins grinned, and K'mith shook his head. "They are crying that this animal of yours is the dog-god, the one the statue is carved to show. And that after all the centuries, the dog-god has repented his evil ways and has come back to do good for all his old harm. There is a prophecy that when the dog-god swims through the water in the belly of a fish and comes into our city with a smile, then all will go well with us as long as he stays. It looks as if you've fulfilled the prophecy, though it didn't say the fish would have atomic power."

He addressed the people briefly, while Muggins grinned. The old man leaned over and whispered into Don's ear. "Three weeks ago, he was telling me these people didn't have no superstitions. Said all this dog-god stuff was just legends they liked to remember because it was in such nice poetry. Now he's telling them he will keep the dog-god for them. Smart boy, this K'mith. He'll never miss a chance to put himself in solid with the voting citizens!"

Cheers were going up as K'mith talked. Finally, some of the more curious came up to examine Shep more closely. The dog growled, but Don shushed him.

K'mith watched for a moment and then went over to the dog. Shep growled again, but relaxed at a word from Don. The Atlantean reached out carefully and stroked the black head as Don had done. Shep sniffed his hand, and finally decided the smell was friendly enough to deserve a halfhearted lick on the fingers. At the sight, a wild cheer went up, and the people began to disperse, as if it had been a sign.

"Yet I have heard often the expression 'mad dog'," K'mith said.

"That means a sick dog." Don tried to describe hydrophobia to the Atlantean, along with assurances that the disease was rare now.

"No wonder the beast was feared," K'mith decided. "But no matter. Even if your Shep were wild, the people want him, and I must obey. You will live with me, then, even as would a child of mine, and you will bring your dog with you to my house. In this emergency, the people must have what comfort they can find. I don't believe the legend; but some of them do."

"Take the offer," Muggins said quickly. "It's the best

chance you'll have. And you'll like the big shot's boy, S'neifa."

Don hesitated. There were advantages in being on good terms with an important man, of course. But it would also mean that he was more carefully watched. He balanced it in his head, uncertainly. Finally, he let it rest on Muggins' words; the old man might or might not be his genuine friend, but he'd have to act as if he were until it was proved one way or the other.

"Thank you," he agreed. "But Shep isn't to be put in a zoo, or anything like that."

"The dog is yours. I ask only the honor," K'mith said formally. "And now, I am finished here. Let's go to your new home."

"What about the others?" the boy asked. "I saw them . . ."

K'mith shrugged. "So I heard. They will be comfortable. And I promise, you will see where they are, later. Come, now."

The city was made up of small streets and houses that looked like blocks of cement, mostly. In spite of their advanced dome, it was almost primitive in many ways. In the center, a few buildings were fairly high. But beyond, everything seemed to be one story high, and no more. With Shep at heel, Don followed K'mith and Muggins toward the residential section, studying the business along the way. He could make no sense of what he saw.

"No money," Muggins agreed. "The city is everyone's father—Mlayanu means Big He in their language. Big He has to support everyone, just the way a father supports his kids. And they have to do what the city—the Council and such—says."

"That sounds like socialism."

"It ain't. It's the family idea, like I said. Because Mlayanu is a real father. He has privileges. He can be nicer to his good children. He gives them a bigger allowance. Works out like money. Some get the best, some get what's left. Only nobody can starve as long as anyone has food. Works pretty good."

Don wondered if having everyone the child of the city of Mlayanu made them all brothers and sisters. But from the bickering going on at the markets, he suspected this wasn't so. "How do they know how much they can afford?"

"They figure it in favors. Man sells you a fish for five favors: you mark it down for him when it reaches a hundred. Then when he has that mark, he goes around to somebody who's done him a hundred favors. Maybe he can even get two hundred favors for your hundred, if you're a big man here. Word gets around how you appreciated the favors, so the new owner won't lose. Works all right here where they've got only about twenty thousand people. Be tough on the surface, though."

Probably it was simple enough in practice. Don gathered that he had a minimum number of favors automatically, and that as one of K'mith's "children" they would have a high value.

They were in the best residential section now, where the Council and other higher-ups lived. The houses still looked like adobe boxes without windows, but they were larger than the ones Don had seen from the outside. Also, they had little strips of ground beside them, about four feet wide and perhaps forty feet long, in which vegetables were growing. Many of the vegetables resembled the ones Don knew from above enough to show that they had come from the surface at one time.

There were men and boys outside some of the houses, who stared in shocked surprise at Shep, and then went quickly inside. Don saw women and girls peeping around the corners at the rear a few seconds later.

They were closer to the submarine than he had thought. As they passed down one narrow little street and turned onto another, he could see the pool ahead, and the submarine lying in it. But now there were a group of Atlanteans around the ship, and men were moving into the ship and out of it. Some of them were carrying instruments.

"They aren't touching the atomics, are they?" he asked sharply.

"Not yet," K'mith answered. "Most of what is in your books and what your men say is pure fantasy. And yet, I have found some truth in it. I am doubtful of the words of caution given by your uncle, Don Miller, but I cannot take chances. Later, in a few days, when we have tested, we shall see."

The submarine was their only chance for escape, Don knew. And it had to be used before the Atlanteans could start fooling with the power plant. They might be able to tackle it without killing everyone, though any who went inside the shielding would die in a short time. But once they released the radiation inside the shields, nobody would be able to use the *Triton* again. It would become a hopeless death trap.

They turned in at one of the houses. K'mith laid one hand on Don's head and another on his wrist. "Enter into the household of Mith, Don K'Miller to be. By the brain that held away the waters, and the hand that built a house within the community of the sea." He smiled. "A superstition, Don—but a pleasant custom, legally binding, enough to make you my son."

A trim-built woman of over forty met them inside the hallway off which the five rooms led. She stepped back quickly, making sure that she did not touch them, and dropped to one knee, then bent until her forehead touched the floor. Behind her, a girl of about twelve did the same.

K'mith ignored the two, and turned to a young man, somewhere between twenty-five and thirty, who stood waiting. "Don K'Miller to be, this is my only son who was born to my brother. He is already honored in the middle education, and is S'neifa."

"Hello, Don," the younger man said. "Don't mind all this. Father and I don't agree, but I've read all I can about your world. I'm glad to see someone from it." He stuck out his hand quickly.

Then he bent over to whisper. "And don't try to understand our family life, any more than I can understand that in your books. My—uh, my mother and sister—*peshna verdon, Mlayanu*—they'll act like slaves in your *Uncle Tom's Cabin*. But we're all equal before Mlayanu. Sometimes it is my father and I who must be slaves."

From the look K'mith threw him, the whispering hadn't been low enough, and the use of the words "mother" and "sister" must be some kind of a violation of basic rules. But nothing was said. The men sat at the table, including Muggins. The woman and girl began to serve the food, always from a kneeling position, and being careful not to touch the men. But they were laughing happily together back at their own hidden table a few minutes afterward. And later Don saw K'mith go back and drop to the same kneeling position while saying something. He heard the woman's voice murmuring, and then saw K'mith come back frowning.

"I cannot show you what I intended," he said. "I am not permitted to take more time with you. S'neifa." He broke into Atlantean words, and S'neifa nodded. The younger man repeated the same performance, and this time it was the girl who answered, in English.

"It is permitted," she said quietly. "I have no fault with you today."

The two women had apparently never seen Don or Shep. Yet the dog came from under their table, licking his chops. Don grinned. The food had been fish in various forms again, with a few vegetables—but it had been well cooked. "Lucky dog," he told Shep, and heard a titter from the girl.

S'neifa blushed, and led Don out quickly. They went down the street, and slightly back toward the business section. Then S'neifa stopped and pointed toward a roof on one of the buildings, surrounded by a low wall. "Look closely, Don. My father K'mith promised you would be shown."

Don strained his eyes, and then made out the faint sign of a separate bubble over the roof. Under it, there were a number of men—men in the clothing of the surface.

The crew of the *Triton* had been put into a prison from which there could be no escape. The only way through the wall of energy that surrounded them was in one of the bubble suits.

He swung on his heel suddenly, intending to knock S'neifa down and head toward the building where his people were. But S'neifa was already heading down the street toward his home. He waved at Don and was gone.

CHAPTER 14/

The Lost People

DON RETURNED TO THE HOME of K'mith after a disappointing visit. He'd been permitted to go up to where his people were, but had not been led through the force-screen dome. And standing outside, making motions had proved an unhappy way to contact them, even when Upjohn had used finger-Morse code. They were comfortable enough, apparently. Kayne was stalking about in nervous anger, and Kenney was lying on a pad, muttering something horrible about bombing the alien spies. The others were accepting the situation, while trying to find some way to get out of it. But all they could suggest to Don was that he play it cautiously, and wait for something to turn up.

He noticed, however, that the dome's phosphorescence was cut at night—apparently during the same hours as night on the surface. That might help, if there was any way to escape.

During the next few days, S'neifa turned out to be a puzzle. He seemed to want to help. K'mith had decided that the books about the surface were full of lies, and nothing could be believed; S'neifa had read them to find on what they agreed, and had checked with Muggins. He had the broad facts about the surface world fairly straight, and mostly made sense. But repeatedly, the conversation ran into snags, where neither could understand the other. Don's description of family life in America left S'neifa slightly ill, and believing that the worst ideas he had dared to have were true—that men and women fought each other through their whole lives, and each was trying to get rid of the other. But Don could only get a vague idea of what went on here, although he had the constant example of the family before him. Affection was strong, but never shown. They took pride in their station, whether male or female, yet spent all their time acting abject. And so far as Don could find out, the men did all the ruling—but the women were complete masters of the men! S'neifa's explanation only muddied things. Don couldn't conceive of a situation where a man could be sent into exile from the family, even while he had the right to forbid the woman to speak at all—where the whole family, including the woman, went into such exile with him! It sounded like nonsense.

He had a somewhat easier time understanding S'neifa's education. The man was in the final stages of his "middle" education, which apparently covered advanced administration and elementary science and technology. His "third" education would come later, where he learned all the technical knowledge of the city. So far as Don could learn from listening, there was no organization or system to it. It was like learning history while studying arithmetic in a Latin book! But it was tough, without much question. No wonder they felt the people under eighteen couldn't take it. Of course, if they hadn't waited until eighteen, it wouldn't have required so much forcing in order to finish during a man's life. S'neifa was twenty-seven and had at least seven more years of study—and he was apparently unusually bright.

Don had always disliked the tight, dry organization and compartmentation of his school books; but now he began to see them as marvels of intelligent presentation of facts. Without them, he might have had to spend the same hard hours of acute labor that S'neifa went through. At times he was tempted to tell the older man that he'd already gone at least as far in school, but this secret was his one ace-in-the-hole, and he hung onto it carefully.

S'neifa took him around the city, finding time for it somehow, and even got him a small, hand-drawn map. It was as strange a mixture as Don had come to expect. They had the marvelous handling of the binding force energies—and by now he knew that the energy of the dome and the energy used in cracking open the submarine were types of energy not used on the surface, but to be found within the nucleus of the atom. Yet, they didn't have atomic energy, nor even a simple steam engine. The propellers that drove the sea sleds were run on electric energy, which came from the most marvelously tiny batteries Don had seen. But they used those motors for nothing else. The general mode of living was probably closer to medieval Europe—except for the cleanliness—than to modern standards; yet in many ways, they had gone far beyond the surface world in science and in government on the local level. The cumbersome-seeming system of favors and paternalistic Mlayanu worked smoothly, and nobody suffered.

S'neifa took it for granted that even a noneducated boy from the surface would know how to build two discs coupled by three fine wires, so that whatever was in front of one could be seen perfectly in the other—with no apparent source of energy. Yet they had never developed television, and the idea that radio wave lengths as short as a few centimeters could exist, was obviously ridiculous to him.

One thing that made an education so difficult was the amount of traditional nonsense they had to learn. Yet Don couldn't help being impressed when S'neifa sat down and drew him a map of Europe as it had been twenty-eight thousand years before. Europe was easily recognizable, too, though Don knew that none of their books showed maps of any sort from the surface.

"We wandered around a lot, the stories say," S'neifa told him. "We were an outcast people—we had split with the totems—is that the word for tribal symbols?— the totems of our tribe. They were using some animal, and we took the fish as a totem, because of a whale that was washed up and saved us in what was a great miracle. And we had the wolf as a totem—the dog-god in the square is probably from that, because the legends say a wolf ate of the whale with us and did not growl. The tribe cast us out, and we wandered. Here, and here—even into the great cold country."

His finger moved across Greece, down Italy, and lingered near the Pyrenees Mountains. It moved on up the coast of France, and around the Baltic to Finland and Sweden. Then he traced it back to France. "But when we came back, the tribe fought us. And we had found boats then among people in the cold country, and we followed our women to an island. It is gone now."

It was a long, rambling story, filled with all kinds of legendary accounts of heroes—over half of whom were women, Don noticed. But they had found an island with a short slope down into the ocean. And as they spread out, they built further and further out onto that slope, until some of their buildings lay a mile from shore. They learned to pack air in softened bladders and breathe it under water, so they could stay down below the surface as much as fifteen minutes. And they spread still more, while the island slowly sank. There came a time when it was all under the surface. But they stayed there for some reason Don could not understand—something about the demons who used beasts on the mainland. They learned to stand the terrible storms, and make their living from the ocean. And they developed electricity.

"Why not?" S'neifa asked. "We had some metals, even then. And around the sea, things react."

With parts of fish left standing in sea water in the sun, they discovered the first accidental battery. They were quicker to develop things than the other tribes who might have found them and forgotten them. They had to be. The land kept sinking, faster now. They built rafts, and learned to make those rafts mostly from seaweed. From electroplating, they found ways to take small models and grow large parts of metal.

And then a marvelous discovery had come—one of the three or four great accidental discoveries of all history. A crystal was washed up and trimmed by one member to a special shape for a necklace. He strung it with copper wire, and looped the wire around to hold it while he located the other ornaments. Then, while he was gone and it lay there, his child tipped it together with a battery into the ocean. When he came back, there was the little dome around it—and the dome would not give. By lifting the wire, he could make or destroy the dome, but nothing could go through it.

It had been pure luck. The elements of the device had to be just right, and there was not one chance in ten billion of it happening. But he drew a picture and kept the parts. And the next winter before the storm came, he found other crystals and built them all the same. He even found he could make the dome grow larger or smaller by adding more batteries or taking some away. And once up, it took almost no energy to keep the dome going.

By a process of trial and error, he had found that one dome could go through another. So he had a way of getting in and out. And that winter his family and he rested snug and secure on the shallow bottom, while the storms raged above. They nearly smothered half the time for the lack of air, but they managed.

And from that impossible accident, the tribe of Mlayanu had developed, passing on their traditions and their pictures, together with their growing crude sciences. They didn't know why things worked, and sometimes never learned. But they kept whatever did work, and had learned to experiment for new things. They found how to charge their batteries from sunlight, by a special device having two thin films of different metals plated together. They improved their batteries.

"I've seen the batteries," Don acknowledged. "We don't have anything like them."

"We had fifteen—nearer twenty—thousand years to develop them. We had to have good batteries," S'neifa said. "Your peoples have better electric motors, because you developed them earlier than we. Until thirty years ago, we used only compressed-air motors. We never found magnetism for all that time. You had to have magnetism to guide your ships, so you saw it for what it was when you found lodestone. We had no need—and only found it recently."

"But those thermocouples you used to get sun energy turned into electricity—we have some now, but they're pretty weak."

"We still use them. Now we get our energy by burying them near the hot part of a volcano under the sea here and using ocean water on the other side. They would freeze the ground under them, so much heat would they take from the sunlight and turn to electricity."

The volcanic basis of their island had then turned active again, and a great upheaval had sent the pleasant island and its beach all the way back to its old level, far below the surface. The domes had been strong enough to stand the shock, but the people had been afraid of the depth, until they got used to it.

They had moved on, looking for new sources of their precious crystals and beginning to get heat from volcanoes under the ocean. This had meant going deeper and deeper, since some of the best had been in the gorges.

By the time they had nearly crossed the ocean, the barbarian tribes on the surface had begun to use metals and build ships. The sea people had deliberately hidden themselves. They had even tried to pretend that there were no surface people any more.

It was a wreck that had first convinced them that they were not alone in civilization. They found fancy goods on it, and metal tools. By then it was miles up to the surface, and a dangerous trip, since they knew too little about the surface life. But as they looked, they discovered other wrecks, and some were of metal. Among these, they found an early radio set. They knew enough to guess some of its purpose, and the antenna on the wrecked ship indicated that it needed a collector of waves above the surface. They had known nothing of radio before—or magnetism, since this was where they first learned of it—but they managed at least to get it to work to some extent for a while.

It was then that K'mith's elder brother, and the real father of S'neifa—his father, the brother of his father, as he put it—had decided to find and bring back a surface dweller. And they'd learned English from Muggins and the books and broadcasts that they were beginning to pick up.

"Most of the people want to stay isolated still," S'neifa told Don. "I know how you feel about your people being locked up, my younger brother. But my people are afraid that the upper world knows too much and is too dangerous. We have heard of your great bombs and your atomic power. We have even heard that you can defy gravity and float on the air."

"Not exactly defy gravity," Don told him. "We use big planes, something like your sea sleds, and go through the air so fast that it doesn't have time to escape from under the planes before we are gone—or that's one way of explaining it."

"It's still a miracle. And we can't trust people who have learned so fast. So the Council voted that all those from the surface who knew about us and could report must stay here. We asked them to promise never to try to leave, but nobody would promise. So we have them where they are safe."

"It won't work," Don told him. "They'll build more submarines, and even stronger ones. They'll explore every inch of the ocean floor some day. And when they find you, they'll be further ahead than now. S'neifa, there are hundreds of millions of us, and only thousands of you. A few thousands can't possibly invent and discover as fast as hundreds of millions. The longer you put it off, the worse it will be."

S'neifa sighed, and nodded. "I have thought of that. But the Council and the people—they hope that one of your great wars on the surface will end all danger from you. Then we can come out slowly and lead the few who still live to a better life."

"You mean to your kind of life?"

"They mean to this kind of life, of course, but both on the surface and here. I—Don, I don't know. There are things in those books—and . . . Tell me, you have been educated already, haven't you?"

Don's breath caught in his throat, and he sputtered. The question had caught him unprepared. If anyone found that he had a good education and could understand the things he saw here—then he'd be locked up with the others, and there would be no chance to escape.

"Don't answer," S'neifa said slowly. "Education is not only what you know, but how you think. And you think like one who has a great deal of education. I knew this long ago. You can read—and much more."

Reluctantly and fearfully, Don nodded. "About the same stage for my culture as you are for yours. I started school when I was six."

"If I—" S'neifa began, and there was a hungry look in his eyes.

But he didn't complete the sentence. A muffled gasp sounded from beyond the door of the room. S'neifa jerked to his feet and went out the door, already dropping to his knee and beginning to bring his head down. There was a rapid patter of Atlantean. Then S'neifa must have gone out, from the sound of his feet. The girl came in and stood gazing at Don with serious eyes.

He wanted to ask for her silence—but there was no way in which he knew of making an appeal. He bent his head in resignation, until her voice reached his ears. "You are a fool, Don K'Miller to be," she said. "A silly, silly fool. Now I know a secret. A secret, a secret. . . ."

She chanted the last, and suddenly swung and was gone down the room and away. If she were going to tell K'mith . . .

A white-faced S'neifa came into the room, before Don could make up his mind. He shook his head doubtfully. "I—I don't know, Don. She listens a lot—even to my lessons—when she isn't supposed to. She doesn't tell, usually. But sometimes . . ." He dropped it unhappily, and threw a piece of paper-like material down. "Since you can read, look at this. Our radio was active yesterday, and we received the news from the surface."

Don picked it up, and scanned it quickly. Then he groaned and read it through again. It was a brief summary, but it showed that his government had entirely misunderstood the bit of his SOS they had heard. They believed that an enemy nation had attacked the *Triton,* and were demanding satisfaction. The nation they were accusing was angry at being accused. And the strained relations were leading them both straight into the horror of an atomic war. In a few more days, it would surely start!

The only hope for peace lay in his finding some means to escape; and if a twelve-year-old girl told her secret, there was no chance at all!

CHAPTER 15 /

Incomplete Barrier

DON WENT OUT, with Shep trailing behind him. The dog no longer frightened any of the Atlanteans, now that he had been completely identified in their minds with the dog-god who was smiling on them. The people watched, making curious little signs to him. And about the only time they smiled was when they saw him. There was a cloud of gloom over the city, and constant references to some emergency. Don had asked about it, but had been told that it was for adults to worry about, not for children.

He had guessed that it somehow tied into the coming of the *Triton* and their fear of the upper world, but it was only a guess. And right now, he had too many worries of his own to care about it.

He went past the submarine now, stopping to watch the men who were studying it. They were still letting the atomic equipment strictly alone, but everything else was being gone over with a fine-toothed comb. As one of them had told him, they hoped to learn enough from other things about the science of the surface to enable them to figure out how the atomic power plant must work. It was a useless hope, Don knew; the technicians here were clever at doing trial and error invention, and they knew every discovery that their race had ever made, including all about the ones that were no longer

121

of any possible use. But they were too practical. They had never developed a theoretical science—and handling atomics involved a lot of theory, too complicated to figure out from the other things aboard the ship.

The *Triton* was seaworthy, however, which was what Don wanted to know. The rocks that had weighed the ship down had now been removed, and she floated easily. Nothing useful had been taken out. And even the device that created the bubble around her was still attached. One of the men who spoke English saw Don studying it, and moved over.

"We will take it off soon," he said. "After we take out the ship into the water there, and see ourselves how work the motors. You will come along, maybe?"

"When?" Don asked.

"The day after tomorrow, I think."

Don's heart seemed to come up and stick in his throat, but he tried to nod casually, as he moved closer to the device. There would be no chance for an escape, he was sure, with a whole crew of the Atlanteans aboard; they'd be able to cut off their bubble-making gadget at any time if he tried to take the ship up—and without that, even the *Triton* couldn't stand the pressure. But once they had made their test and removed the gadget, there'd be no chance at all of getting the ship through the dome and into the ocean. Escape would *have* to be made somehow before that date.

Then the full idea hit. When they took the ship out, they couldn't test it without cutting off the bubble! Yet the second the bubble was gone, the ship would almost certainly be destroyed by the pressure of the sea!

He could feel the noose being drawn tighter and tighter about his neck, but he tried not to show it as he drew up beside the group of crystals connected to batteries by oddly twisted wires. "How does this work?" he asked.

The technician shrugged. "You press this lever, and it works. More than that, I do not know. It is for the technicians of the power dome to explain. And to them it is a secret, even from us—if they know. Maybe some day, Don K'Miller to be, when you have been educated and are no longer the child, you will become a power-dome technician. Until then . . ."

He shrugged again, and pulled the boy away from the device gently. Don had found a few things, however. The bubble spread over solids, but was stopped by anything liquid, such as water, tarry materials, or glass—which acted like a liquid in many ways. The floor of the prison where the *Triton* crew was kept was of a tarry substance that stopped it. He also knew that it was a lot less simple than it seemed, and that as long as he was considered a child, nobody would talk to him about it.

Yet something kept driving him to find out. With even a small amount of added information, there might be some means of escape. The dome was mixed up in everything—the prisoners were locked in by one, the submarine was immobilized unless one could be thrown around it, and the whole life of the city was wrapped up in it.

He walked glumly toward the building he had spotted before, where the power came in from the volcanic heat plant and was used to create the dome. It was a big round building with a single entrance, and a sign which he knew meant that nobody was allowed in. He had been by a dozen times already, but either the big door had been closed or a technician had been on guard.

But this time, the door seemed to be unlocked, and there was no guard. Don glanced up and down the street, and tapped Shep lightly on the shoulder. "Go home, Shep!" he ordered. The dog whined, but moved away slowly.

No one was around. Don moved up to the door carefully and found it open the barest crack. He stuck his eye to the opening and stared inside, to see a huge room filled with aisles and rows of complicated crystals and a maze of wiring. Far down at one end there was the mutter of worried voices, and he could see movement as someone would occasionally pass across an opening. But whatever was going on was taking up most of their attention.

With a prayer for luck, he moved inside, sliding along the wall and holding his breath as he came to a section of open space. He moved from hiding place to hiding place, studying the big installation as he went. After his years of studying electronics, he had thought that no complicated device could be totally meaningless to him. He was wrong—nothing worked at all like anything he knew.

Then he came to a section that did make sense— because it had been assembled from bits of radio equipment and duplicated parts. But it was disconnected now. He started on, then stopped as he saw a diagram there. The Atlanteans used symbols entirely different from the ones he knew, but with the device itself, he could learn what the various curlicues meant. He tried to photograph it in his mind, before moving on. Another section of Atlantean work had one of their diagrams fastened to it, and he studied that. This time it made sense.

One of the technicians came down the aisle then, barely giving Don warning by the sound of his feet. The man hurried along as Don pulled himself under a table; in the bundle he carried were scraps of paper-like material, scrawled over. He dumped them into a box and hurried back. Don let out a sigh of relief and moved forward to pick up the marked-up diagrams.

The sharp bark of a dog echoed in the big chamber suddenly, and Shep came bounding along the aisle, straight toward Don. The boy gasped, realizing what a fool he'd been. Shep hadn't been here long enough to consider K'mith's house home. He'd only been confused by Don's order. And now he was back.

Don heard a shout collecting from the technicians and the sound of heavy feet pounding down the aisles. He leaped for the diagram, scooped it up and pocketed it, and then darted away. Ahead there was the flicker of movement. He ducked into a side aisle, with Shep leaping along.

"Get out, Shep!" he whispered. The dog hesitated, then dashed out. Some of the technicians spotted him and gave chase. Don ducked into another aisle, under a table, and down the main aisle toward the door. He saw Shep bounce through, and then was dashing for it himself. He saw someone behind him, but there was no chance to look back. He hit the door, slammed it after him, and darted around a corner, zigzagging through the streets. Behind him, he heard a hue and cry, but for the moment he was safe.

He was sure they couldn't prove he'd been the one in the dome station—but the presence of Shep was suspicious enough. It wouldn't do to go back to K'mith; and the only other place he could think of was the prison. It would give him an excuse for being out, and Muggins might back up his story.

Muggins grinned when he heard Don's hasty account, however. "Nope. You're a child, remember. Don't matter if you do go in there, so long as you don't touch anything. They probably didn't bother looking at you— just wanted to get your dog out before he could get into something. Look, I gotta take food in." He was fastening on the bubble device that permitted him to enter the little dome, and now he winked broadly. "Don't you touch me before I put on power, or you'll be in the bubble, too."

A second later, with Don touching his shoulder and the bubble of force spread out over both of them, he walked through the dome. He snapped off power, put down the food, and turned it on again to leave, pretending not to notice that Don had gotten inside the prison dome.

There was a wild hubbub then, as Simpson rushed up to him and the others followed. His uncle looked thin and sick. "Off my feed," he explained quickly. "The diet here doesn't agree with my ulcers."

It took Don five minutes to answer their questions and assure them that he was all right. Then he had to report on the situation, and they sobered. There seemed to be no way in which they could possibly escape before the submarine was in a condition where it would be useless to them. Yet they had to get out before that time.

Kenney had hovered around, but now he grumbled miserably and stomped back to his cot. "Had a run-in with K'mith this morning," Upjohn explained. "He's still fighting mad. K'mith probably is, too."

But this time it was Drake whom Don most wanted to see. He drew the physicist aside, with his uncle joining them, and spread out the diagram he had found, explaining what he had decoded from the others. Even the most complicated electronic device uses only a few different basic parts, and it was easier to decode than might have been thought. Drake found a sheet of paper in Upjohn's coat pocket and began retracing the diagram with Don's help.

Part of it was peculiar, but the basic setup was familiar to Don. "It's like a signal generator—it simply feeds in several different frequencies to control something. But what?"

It was an hour later when Drake finally shrugged. "I still don't know how it all works, but I think we're right. We know they can control this screen to let through anything from nothing at all through light, and finally spread it thin enough for gas to come through. This is what does it. If they feed in no signal at all, absolutely nothing at all—no matter what it is or at what pressure—can get through. With the right frequency, they can pick what they want. They must have been trying to tune it properly, because I've notice the thing has flickered a few times lately."

"Anything at all?" Don asked. "Then if the atom bomb were to hit this . . . ?"

Drake blinked, and suddenly nodded. "You're right! They could set this so a million H-bombs wouldn't matter. Great Harry, if we had this . . . We've got to have it! Put up a screen around every city in the world, and war wouldn't be possible—or matter. Don, get back out there, and get twice as busy as you can. We've got to get this back to the surface!"

Don nodded. He'd been thinking the same. He grabbed his uncle's hand quickly, and then motioned for Muggins. The old man came through in a bubble, chuckling. He began muttering false surprise at finding Don inside the bubble, and made contact. Ten seconds later, Don was heading back to the street. It had occurred to him that one of the others might be of more use outside, but he knew it was false. Muggins wouldn't have released anyone else—he'd have used his weapon first; and Don was the only one who had a chance to move around freely. For that matter, even if Muggins had been willing to let them out, he wouldn't have dared.

Shep was waiting for him outside, and he headed back to the house of K'mith. His newly adopted father came out to meet him with a sheaf of papers, but there was no anger on the man's face. If the guards had spotted Don at the plant, they must have let it go, as Muggins had said.

"You look excited," K'mith said mildly.

Don caught himself, but the idea that had been taking shape wouldn't hold back. "I've been talking to Drake and my uncle. K'mith, there isn't any reason to be afraid of the surface now! Your screen—it can be set to protect you from the bomb completely. It can—"

K'mith smiled faintly. "I know, Don K'Miller to be. We found what the radiation was from your ship, and the technicians are tuning the dome to handle it now. But there are new developments."

Don suddenly felt silly. His triumph couldn't have fallen flatter. And yet, if K'mith knew they were safe . . . He looked at the paper the older man held out, frowning. It was another bulletin that summarized news received over their radio listening branch. The United States had given the foreign nation an ultimatum—five days to return the *Triton* unharmed or make reparations; and the other country had replied in a frenzy of angry denial, and given *four* days for a complete retraction, or what amounted to full war.

Don gasped. He had no idea the relations were that strained. He tried to imagine a world plunged into the holocaust of atomic war in another four or five days. But it seemed impossible.

"Then you've got to let the *Triton* go, sir," he said.

"You wouldn't want to have war up there, would you? And now that you're completely safe here—"

"Nations only fight nations because they are filled with fear and hate," K'mith said quietly, but there was pain on his face. "If they had been friendly, nobody would have thought a missing ship was attacked by an *enemy*. The war is not our responsibility. I tried to explain this to your Senator Kenney, and he argued as you do, for a time. And he has convinced me of that hatred. I do not mind being called a spy, murderer, and other things. But I do mind when a representative of your government tells me he will have poison dropped to kill all the life in our waters, on which we eat, and so many H-bombs that no one will ever know there was a valley here."

"But—" Don began.

K'mith put a hand on his shoulder. "Let me finish. You are still a child. But believe me, we do not have a complete barrier. There is one thing which can always come through. And that is hate! So long as hate exists above, we can only exist here by secrecy. And because of that, I must keep your friends prisoners. And I must forbid you ever to see them again, or to go near our dome-control plant. Tonight, see your friends and bid them a brief good-by. Then forget them. And I wonder—is even isolation not an incomplete barrier to such hatred?"

Don studied K'mith's face, and then turned to his and S'neifa's room sickly. He couldn't even find a convincing argument.

CHAPTER 16/

Stranded in Atlantis

DON WAS LYING IN DARKNESS when S'neifa came into the room. He had learned that the cold light from the ceilings could be cut off, and he didn't want to look at anything while his mind was torn with the impossible need to answer an impossible riddle. The only hope for the world above was for the *Triton* to escape with the secret of the dome. And there was nothing he could do about it. He was in a worse position than before.

S'neifa turned the light up to a faint twilight and dropped onto the cot beside Don. His face was strained, as if he had fought a battle within himself. "She hadn't told," he said. He fidgeted, but Don could think of nothing to say. Then he dragged out a small bundle and handed it to Don. "I—I don't agree with my father K'mith, Don. I think we cannot have separate worlds. Like you, I think we have to learn to live together. Yet it's hard to disobey, to be a traitor to my city, when I may be wrong. I—oh, take it! It's a personal shield generator. You can wear it under your clothes and take your friends through the prison dome. I'll have the controls on your submarine set, and I'll turn on the bubble when you turn the periscope pickup toward the stern. Nobody works on the submarine at night, anyhow."

He hid his face as Don stumbled to find words. His voice was muffled. "Don't thank me, Don K'Miller who

129

is not to be. I did it because something within me made me; I spent the whole afternoon at the temple, trying to be true to the gods of my fathers in whom I have never believed. And yet—there is the control. With it is a scroll showing the principles of the dome. What more can you want?"

Don sat with the package in his hands, staring at the other. He'd been striking up blind alleys for days—and now S'neifa had given him everything, without being asked. "I guess more than hate comes through the barrier," he said at last. "It looks as if something called love for fellowmen comes through, too. But I'm sorry if it makes you feel like that."

"Don't be." S'neifa sat up, and reached for the light control, brightening it. "I'm all right now, Don. I guess I'm glad I made up my mind." He grinned, wryly. "You'd better get going. My father K'mith says you're permitted to see your people tonight, and it's dark out already. I'll be at the *Triton*. Remember the signal!"

He reached out for Shep and scratched the dog's ears. Shep bobbled his tail happily, and stood up to lick S'neifa's face.

"S'neifa," Don said. He caught his breath, and then plunged ahead. Like the other's action, this was something that hurt, but it would have been worse not to do it. "S'neifa, you keep Shep. You can call him sort of a hostage, if you like. But I want you to have him."

The Atlantean grinned slowly, and stuck out his hand. Don took it quickly, picked up the package, and headed out.

There was a dim twilight on the streets, as there was always at night here. Don was glad of it, since no one would see his expression before he got control of himself. He heard S'neifa close the door behind him, as the other went down toward the *Triton* to do his part of the job, and then Don quickened his steps.

Muggins wasn't on duty at night. There was another guard, and one who apparently didn't speak English. But he had been notified that Don could come. Don could feel the bulges under his jacket where he had the generator strapped, but apparently the other didn't notice. He nodded, and stepped back to let the young man walk up to the screen.

Don wasted no time. He reached out his hand for the guard, as if handing him something. The guard automatically lifted his own hand. As they touched, Don snapped on his screen.

The man's surprise was just what he'd been counting on. He slapped one hand over the weapon in the other's holster, and yanked with the other. The guard stumbled, and they were across the barrier. Don snapped the generator off at once and let out a yell.

Upjohn had caught on that something was wrong at once. Now he jumped forward instantly. One of his fists moved through a short arc, before the guard could turn. It caught the man on the chin, and dropped him. Don stooped down and recovered the weapon, then felt to see if the guard were wearing a bubble-generator. He wasn't.

The blow hadn't knocked him completely unconscious. He got up quickly, backing away and shouting. But sound didn't spread through the dome barrier, and no one outside could have heard.

Don motioned him back toward the opposite side of the dome, and reached for Upjohn's necktie. The reporter jerked it off and began tying the guard's hands and feet together. "Spill the news," he suggested, "while I tie this."

Don told them about it as quickly as he could, warning about the probability of guards below, and stressing the signal that would get S'neifa to turn on the generator for the *Triton*. They'd have to turn on the jets briefly to pick up a slight forward motion, then signal. He'd have just time enough to put on the bubble when they cut the jets, and they'd go drifting out through the city dome and into the ocean.

There they would be lighter than the water, now that the rocks were removed, and would rise rapidly. Someone would have to go out in the bathysuit, and cling to the hull while he turned off the bubble device, if they wanted to maneuver. But there would probably be no harm if they left it on until they surfaced. Then anyone could go out through an escape hatch and cut it off, where no pressure would bother him.

"I like the scheme," Haller agreed. "It has the one advantage none of the plans we cooked up here had. It's simple and direct. And the best tricks always are. Well, we've got one weapon, at least. But how are we all going to get through this barrier?"

"You'll just have to join hands. The field around me will cover all of you," Don said. He'd thought this through on the way from K'mith's house, and he was sure it would work.

Haller nodded, and reached for his hand. The others fell into line, leaving Kayne and Kenney at the end. The Senator was suddenly glowing, bubbling with good spirits, while explaining just what he would have done to the Atlanteans once they got back.

"Better forget it," Haller advised him curtly. "Don't overlook the fact that it was an Atlantean who made this escape possible."

Kenney blinked, and nearly shut up. He mumbled something to Kayne, who nodded nervously.

Then they were all in line, and Don cut on the generator. He couldn't see the bubble in the dimly lighted air, but he started for the main dome. There was no resistance. He held hands while the others came through, without trouble. Finally, when all were out, he let the generator stop, and they released each other.

"What about the guard?" his uncle whispered. "He wasn't a bad keeper. He did his best to treat us well."

"He won't be hurt," Haller decided. "Muggins will find him in the morning and let him out. And he'll be better off if we leave him that way. At least, he can prove he was overcome."

They grouped together at the head of the stairs. Don handed the weapon over to Haller, who took it. There might be guards below, but they couldn't be sure.

Don started down first, since he would be expected. But now, to confuse the issue, he turned on the bubble.

If a guard had sharp eyes, he'd see it and be suspicious. And nothing could hurt Don as long as he wore it. If he could draw their fire, Haller could locate them and take care of the situation.

Don stumbled on the stairs. The bubble stayed a quarter of an inch from his skin, as it was set, and made it seem that he was walking on absolutely frictionless ice. He caught the handrail, but that only helped a little.

He grumbled to himself, but then realized it would be even better for his purposes—if he could get down at all, without breaking his neck. Skidding and fighting for control, he went down the steps. It was a strange sensation to be expecting fire at any moment, even though he knew he was safe.

But nothing happened. He reached the bottom and stepped onto the street, turning off his generator. "All right," he called back softly. "Come on."

Out of the darkness behind him a tiny red point glowed for a fraction of a second. Don dropped on his face, and something spatted over him. Almost at the same time, there was a faint hiss from the stairs.

Haller jumped forward and spun toward a doorway, yanking it open. A paralyzed guard dropped out, his stungun falling from his hands. "Smart," Haller said. "A good man. He waited until he saw what you would do next, instead of firing at once. Figured you must have some plan under your bubble. I'd like to have a lot like him under me. Well, they'll fix him up when they find him. Take his gun, Sid. You're next best shot."

"Better break up," Don suggested. "Mostly at this hour, there are only small groups of Atlanteans around. We'll be conspicuous enough in our clothes, without calling attention to ourselves."

"Good idea. You say this street leads straight to the submarine? Then if we break up and a few take this street, some the one below, and some the one above, we'll all get there without needing a guide."

Surprisingly, Kayne broke away first, drawing Kenney with him. They went up the street, and turned toward the submarine. Haller broke the others up into two groups, putting Upjohn at the head of one and taking the other himself, together with Don.

They began moving along quietly and without too much speed. Fortunately, almost nobody seemed to be on the street, and they were apparently attracting no attention. They moved almost halfway to the submarine before there was a sudden yell from the next street where Upjohn had gone.

"Come on!" Haller yelled. They shot around the corner and headed for the other group. Haller's judgment had been sound. They came out behind the group facing the men with Sid Upjohn.

There were only six of them, but two seemed to be guards armed with stunguns. Sid had scattered his group into doorways, and was shouting for help. As he saw Haller and the others he shut up and began firing busily.

Haller motioned for the others to take cover, but began moving forward himself in the open. He was reciting some piece of nonsense verse in a voice that sounded as if he was giving orders. Both guards immediately swung around. One of them dropped from a quick shot as Sid Upjohn darted out of the doorway, and Haller had already pinpointed the other.

The other four went into a mad scramble for the guns, but the group from the *Triton* was on them at once. The odds were too uneven. The Atlanteans never had a chance, and it was over in a few seconds.

"Thanks, Bob," Upjohn said quietly. "Now let's beat it."

The doors along the way were beginning to open and citizens were poking reluctant heads out. It was time to move. Most of the people would be cautious about coming out in the face of gunfire, but some fool might go charging in, and touch off the others. Haller nodded, and they began to run down the street. It was barely in time. Atlanteans came boiling around the corner behind them.

But there were no guns among them. The men from the *Triton* went down the street at a steady clip. Then the doors ahead began to pop open, attracted by the noise. People were moving out all along the little street, threatening to block the way.

Haller motioned, and they turned a corner and then ducked into the street where his group had originally been, on a direct line to the submarine. There were still a few curious open doors, and he motioned them over to the street where Kayne and Kenney had gone.

It was clear sailing there, unless someone should be smart enough to guess that they would head for the submarine. And Don didn't think most of the people would have any idea of what was going on. He began to breathe easier.

Then they came to the end of that street, two short blocks up from where the *Triton* lay. They swung back, losing a few more seconds. There had been no sign of Kenney or Kayne, who must have gone on ahead, unless they had been caught while the noise from the first fight was distracting everyone.

They swung onto the main street—and ahead lay the *Triton*. Light was streaming out of the open hatch.

"Come on," Haller repeated, and doubled his speed.

Don gasped suddenly. The *Triton* was already moving faintly, and a jet of spray was lancing up from the pool where the smallest power of her jets was kicking out the water. As he watched, she began drifting straight toward the edge of the dome.

"Wait!" The voice was that of Dexter, raised to a roar Don would have thought impossible to the man. He added his own yells, but the ship went on. Then the hatch snapped down sharply.

There was a bobbing of the periscope pickup, and suddenly a dim bubble appeared around the *Triton*. She seemed to rise several inches, and then touched the barrier of the dome and went drifting through, out into the ocean.

When part-way through, the lifting of her bow sent her through more rapidly. She suddenly leaped upward, and was gone!

Don saw S'neifa dropping back from the pool and

staring at him in open-mouthed surprise. The Atlantean had been at the bubble control, where he couldn't see what was happening, and where he'd been safe from the spray. But now he stopped.

"Run!" Don yelled.

It was too late. Men were appearing from all sides. S'neifa was caught before he could move. And behind, Don heard the mob coming toward his group.

"Throw down the guns," Haller said. "We're licked."

But his face was sicker than mere defeat would account for, and Don felt the same. Kayne and Kenney had gone, leaving them hopelessly stranded.

CHAPTER 17/

The Judgment of K'mith

FROM THE ROOFTOP where they were all imprisoned within the dome, they could see the pool where the *Triton* had been, and could see the men moving out on sea sleds, equipped with supply bubbles. It was an emergency expedition, and the supplies they carried would include air for a trip to the surface and back if they needed it. There seemed to be an endless stream of Atlanteans as they watched.

S'neifa was one of their own group now. He sat hunched over, staring at the pool bitterly. He'd blamed himself for the blunder, though he had actually followed the plan perfectly and couldn't be condemned. But all his doubts about the idea were now boiling within him. He was branded a traitor—and a failure as one.

"Maybe they'll make it," Haller said doubtfully. "They've been gone quite a while. But I wish they'd at least waited for that book on the dome. That hurts. All they can do now is to report us. And at this stage, I don't think the return of the *Triton* is enough to stop the war that's coming. The dome secret would have done it."

"What good would the book have done without someone who knew the meaning?" Don asked.

Haller smiled bitterly. "You'd be surprised. Knowing it was electronics, they'd have treated it as a special code, and the boys would have cracked it in hours. They do things like that every day."

Bitterness lay too deep in the others for talk. The idea that one of their group would deliberately desert them seemed impossible to swallow.

Then Haller signaled. "Something happening."

They crowded against the low ledge around the roof, where the dome had been spread out to give them a chance to use it. There was feverish excitement around the edge of the pool, and men were dropping in and swimming off into the ocean beyond in droves, but now without the supply tanks.

A man shot through the other way, and began waving excitedly. There was no sound through the barrier around the roof, but they could see the crowd stand up and begin to cheer. Haller nodded curtly. A second later, a dim shadow sprang into view and began sliding down toward the edge of the dome near the pool. It was the *Triton* without any question, still encased in the bubble.

There were no rocks this time, they saw. The ship was being dragged down by the numbers who swam along beside her, dragging on the tangle of ropes around her. Her flotation couldn't overcome the steady pull of the little sleds that were dragging her down. As the men on the roof watched, the nose of the ship came through the big dome, and a second later she was back in the pool.

Men went through her bubble at once, and it snapped off. Others brought up equipment and tackled the hatch, which came open a few minutes later. In almost no time, the figures of Kenney and Kayne were dragged out.

"When I get my hands on them," Walrich began.

Haller shook his head. "We do nothing. That's an order. We can't have rioting among ourselves. Our standing in this city is poor enough now. Coventry is good enough."

It was half an hour later when the two men were shoved through the dome. Kenney was screaming. He took one look at the men, clutched his heart, and scrambled for his pallet. "I'm an old man. I had to get back. My country needs me. I'm not expendable."

"Save it for your conscience," Haller said curtly. "And since I know you still have one, that's enough. Mr. Kayne, you will consider yourself under arrest. The charge is deserting in the face of the enemy, mutiny, piracy, and anything else I can decide on later. But first, I want a report, without an alibi."

The nervous navigator tried to be defiant, and couldn't make it. "We got to the surface," he said. "They came right up after us. We couldn't get rid of the screen before they were there. And there weren't enough of us to handle the ship." He twisted his hands and again tried to brazen it out. "What would you have had me do? Did you want to lose what chance there was, just because you couldn't stay out of brawls?"

"That will do, Mr. Kayne," Haller ordered. "You had time to wait. Kindly retire to your bunk and remain there."

Kayne doubled his fists nervously. Haller took half a step forward, then stopped. But the navigator went to his bunk and remained there in silence.

The jail building was surrounded by a group of Atlanteans, pointing up. Apparently they expected something to happen on the roof, and were surprised when quiet reigned.

Muggins came in with food for them. "Trial will be tomorrow," he said. "I ain't supposed to talk to you. Dratted fools. But with the right kind of men, you'd have made it, Admiral. Wish I'd had men like you over me in the old days."

"The plan was Don's," Haller told him. "I only executed it. And I should have allowed for the men under me. Give him the credit, and I'll take the blame, if there is any. How are they taking it down there?"

"The Council's in a real tizzy. All except K'mith. He's just put on a green suit."

S'neifa let out an anguished wail, and his face whitened. He doubled up and began crying, without trying to hide it.

"Means he's mourning the death of his son," Muggins said. "He's declaring S'neifa publicly dead. It's kind of tough on the President of the Council having a boy who acts like a traitor, seems."

Haller frowned. "K'mith's the ruler here?"

"Sort of. Thought you knew. The Council can veto him, but otherwise he's practically king of the city. Guess that makes Don the prince, since he's not been declared dead yet. K'mith will be sitting on your case tomorrow."

He went out, taking the nearly full plates with him. No one had been hungry. Haller and Simpson went over to S'neifa, trying by silent companionship to help. Don went last, but he had no idea of what to do. At last he put his hand on the other's shoulder and left it there. S'neifa put his own hand over it. It seemed silly and sentimental to Don and yet somehow right.

They sat up through most of the night, saying almost nothing. When the lights in the city began to brighten, indicating that day had arrived, they were still sitting in nearly the same positions they had been in hours before.

Muggins came back with only the bitter herb drink that was their morning wake-me-up. Then he dumped it quietly down a drain, and pulled out a huge container. "Coffee. I got someone to bring it off the ship. They figure it's something intoxicating, so you're not supposed to have it. But I figured you'd need it—you too, S'neifa. No milk, but . . ."

"You're a prince, Muggins," Upjohn told him. "How about yourself?"

Muggins poured, and nodded. "Don't mind if I do. Here's how." He smacked his lips, and his eyes rolled upward. "If you only knew how many years I useta lie thinking about coffee, dreaming about it. . . ."

S'neifa gagged over the bitter stuff, but he swallowed it. And since he was unused to it, the stimulus of it hit him quickly. He brightened a little.

Muggins waited, and then nodded. "Okay, I guess we might as well get down and into the business of the day. You ready to have K'mith come up and judge you?"

"Here?" Don asked. He'd expected to be led out into the street under guard and into some crowded hall where justice was handed out.

"Easier than taking you down," Muggins said. "They do things the simple way here. Ready?"

Haller shrugged and nodded. "As well have it now as any time."

Muggins went through the dome. A moment later, guards began coming in, their weapons ready. They lined up along the wall, circling the men.

Finally K'mith came through, with a scribe behind him, who would write it all down, and five other men who would apparently act as witnesses of the trial, making sure that nothing was done improperly. There were no lawyers.

K'mith was dressed in a bright shade of green, but there was no expression of sorrow or anything else on his face. He shook hands with Haller. "A very nice try, Admiral. Naturally, we couldn't let it succeed. But you handled your men well."

Then he smiled at Don. "And I must admit, so did you, Don who was to be K'Miller. But it seems you have chosen sides too strongly for me to influence you. Yet, since there was no disgrace in what you did, it is a strong pleasure in my old age to know that I still have a son in you. A man needs at least one son. As K'mith for Mlayanu, I find you have committed something I cannot permit. But as K'mith of my household, I am not displeased with your conduct."

He did not look at S'neifa. And when Kenney began threatening what would happen, K'mith nodded to one of the guards, who moved forward, signaling for silence with his gun. The old man quieted, terror heavy in his eyes.

"This court of judgment will now begin," K'mith said quietly. "Please be seated around me that you may hear my judgment." He waited while the guards motioned the others into a semicircle, then seated himself at the hub of it. "Our practices here are not the same as those above the sea, from what little I can learn. I have determined the facts already. There will be no trial. As I know those facts, you broke from your prison and attempted to flee, against my former judgment on you. This applies to all but my son Don, who freed you and then joined you—and he who was the son of my brother K'mayo, who betrayed us of the city of Mlayanu. These are the facts. But out of courtesy, if they are not true as you see them, I will listen."

"They're true," Haller agreed. Kenney sprang up with a scream, threshing the air with his fists.

"I won't stand for this travesty of a trial. I shall not be a party to such a gross perpetration of rank injustice. First, I claim diplomatic immunity. Second I—"

"Silence him," K'mith said quietly. A guard pushed the old man down gently, and tapped his stungun significantly. Senator Kenney sank back, casting an appealing glance at Haller, who shrugged.

"Thank you, Admiral Haller," K'mith said. "As you know, our rules are different. But you *are* in our city, and we have to try you as we know justice. I have been considering this judgment through the night."

He paused, and pulled out a scroll, reading down the names of everyone there except S'neifa and Don. "We find that the safety of Mlayanu demands a closer guard on these," he said quietly. "Their imprisonment shall now be officially for life, save that in the case of such an emergency as we now have grave reason to fear, they shall be left to the mercy of the sea before others of the city. The submarine, *Triton,* upon which they came, shall be permanently disabled by the removal of all devices to protect it with a field of force, and by the further removal of all valves to those tanks which hold water, to assure that this submarine shall sink if rashly moved into the seas around us. Imprisonment for you shall be further enforced by cementing the force field on the outside with rock through which no man may enter, and by leaving only an opening the size of a small man's head in the flooring, through which sustenance and waste may be passed. No man of Mlayanu shall converse with the prisoners at any time.

"To Don Miller, our son, we forbid our household until such time as he may be deemed fit to return. And we order that he be placed in a small room and heavily guarded. He shall be treated as one who may eventually be of service to Mlayanu, and shall be given consideration for the possession of one dog, Shep, which has become of value to the city.

"And to the former son of K'mayo, my brother, there shall be this: He shall live in the house of the brother of his father, but shall not speak to any man from now until the day he shall die, unless he can win forgiveness of his city by some act which shall make all forget the day of darkness. He shall be known as Arain Neifa, and he shall be the servant of the household in which he resides, or of any other to which he may be sold, being rated as the lowest among the laboring class. And once each day at noon, he shall walk the length of the city with his eyes to the ground, that all may see his example."

K'mith stood up. "That is all."

Don jumped to his feet. "I appreciate your giving me special consideration, sir," he said—which wasn't true, since it had made him feel like a fool and a heel among the others. "But I do not deserve it. I'd like to be locked up with the others."

"You misunderstood," K'mith said. "I was not meaning to give you special consideration. As my son, you merit special punishment. It was my belief that by taking you away from all your friends here and locking you away by yourself, your punishment would be greater. You confirm this. Therefore, the judgment stands."

He shook hands with Haller again, and rubbed his hand affectionately over Don's head. Then he snapped on his bubble and went through the screen, with the guards following him. One guard took S'neifa by the arm. The young man staggered as he walked, but he shook off the guard and moved stolidly forward.

Don turned to his uncle, trying to smile. There were tears in Simpson's eyes. Their hands met very briefly, but neither could think of anything to say.

Then he went out with the guards, trying not to cry.

CHAPTER 18 /

Emergency Plans

IMPRISONMENT wasn't too drastic. Don found that he was simply locked in a large room in the building where he had first come to, and that there were double doors, between which a guard stayed with a stungun. Muggins was still his keeper, along with the guard whom he had tricked. The latter didn't exactly regard him with great favor, but didn't show any signs of taking a bad feeling out on him.

He was given games to play—most of them much too simple—and the best of food. But after one day of that, time hung heavy on his hands. He had enough to think about, but none of it was pleasant. He'd been responsible for the plans the others followed. They had come from S'neifa originally, and been executed by Haller. But he was still responsible.

And meanwhile, the situation above wasn't improving any. He was indirectly responsible for that. It wasn't good to think about.

He woke the second day with the determination that he was going to escape. He had no idea of how at first, beyond a faint notion that there must be a way to use Shep to get out of this. But somewhere during the night, he'd stopped worrying about things and fretting through self-recrimination. It was his duty to get them all out, and he meant to do it.

He grinned at himself bitterly as he realized he had somehow adopted the attitude that must be normal for Haller, without all of Haller's experience. Yet there must have been some time when Haller had been forced to take the same line without experience. It gave him a measure of confidence to know that it could be done.

"I'm bored," he told Muggins. "Can you get me a small tube of metal, a pair of pliers, and a file—just a small file. I've been thinking of making tin whistles."

"You've been plotting," Muggins said grimly. He scratched his gray head and thought it over. "I don't like the look in your eyes now, youngster. But still, I'm durned if I can see how you can cause any trouble with that. Unless you want to make a bean-shooter, and that won't hurt many too much. All right, I'll get 'em."

When the tools came, he went to work. He'd had a supersonic whistle for Shep, which gave out sounds too high for a human ear to hear. The dog, however, could hear them over a great distance. He tried to remember how the whistle had been made. He finally had to sit down and figure it out from the theory of resonant circuits he'd had in training. It might be the wrong approach, but it might work.

The first one turned out to be a fairly good whistle, except that it sounded something like a screech owl howling at night. He threw it aside and began bending and filing another, this time with the idea of filing it down until he could barely hear the faintest high sound, and then modifying that again to be a trifle higher.

K'mith came by once and looked in without a word while he was in the middle of work. But he didn't question Muggins' having given the materials to him. Muggins watched from the peephole outside with considerable fascination. "Too bad we don't have willows, youngster," he remarked. "I used to be pretty good at making willow whistles and flutes. Could even play something like a tune on 'em. Get a nice octave jump, too, by blowing hard."

"Thanks, Muggins," Don said. He'd been missing the fact that a whistle will give two notes. One comes from gentle blowing, while hard breathing will produce a note just twice as high in frequency. If he tuned his whistle for about ten or eleven thousand cycles a second—maybe a little higher—and then jumped the octave, it should work perfectly.

He went back to the one he had been trying to modify and tested it with low breathing. He filed a little more from it. This time when he tried, it seemed to be about right. With a long intake of breath, he forced in wind as hard as he could. There was a faint whine at first, and then it was silent.

He tried again, without results. But the fifth time, there was a loud bark below, and he laughed quietly to himself. "Better let Shep in," he told Muggins.

"Can't," the man said. But he frowned. "You're doing that, though I'll be switched if I know how. Well, it's between you and the dog."

Don heard Shep's feet scratching at the door and the voice of the guard trying to chase him away. It went on for a while, until half an hour later K'mith showed up and took the protesting dog away. An hour later, Don was packed up and moved to new quarters.

He began on the whistle again, and this time it was the other guard who watched. "What's going on?" he asked in Atlantean.

Don shrugged. "God talk," he said, in a few words of Atlantean he had learned. "Hear god come."

Shep was wilder this time. There was a peephole with bars lower down, and the dog jumped up to it. Around his throat was a chain that clanked on the floor.

K'mith didn't look happy when he came the second time. He held a long conversation with the guard and finally came in for the whistle. Don gave him the first one that hadn't worked. As he went out, the boy blew on the supersonic one. There was a surprised cry, and Shep was back.

K'mith looked more perturbed. And again Don was moved, with the same results. This time, Don waited an hour after K'mith had collected the dog. He'd heard the babble of voices below—voices that were considerably perturbed. To the superstitious part of the population, such behavior on the part of their dog-god must be disturbing, to say the least.

When Don finally began whistling again, Shep didn't come. But after a few minutes, a low, mournful wailing began to keen through the air. Don could just hear it by listening carefully. Shep had given up trying to break free of whatever held him, and was using the ghostly wail he sometimes had used at the moon on lonely nights on the island. He had a bay that would have made a hound-dog jealous.

Muggins came in about half an hour later, and spoke to the guard. Then he unlocked the door, and motioned Don out. "All right, youngster. K'mith is a stubborn man, but half the people are claiming the emergency is here, and the dog is warning them. They're scared sick, and K'mith says to come back at once and keep that dog quiet."

Don got up and followed Muggins. He'd been right about one thing at least. Instead of using his own strength, the trick was to use the weakness of the others. Atlantis had a superstitious people, and that was one weakness. There were others.

"What's all this emergency stuff, Muggins?" he asked. "I've been hearing about it all the time, but nobody will tell me. Is it the fear that our ships will come down and bomb them?"

Muggins' face had darkened with worry. "Older than that. It's what happened to all the other domes. They tell me that at one time, there were twelve domes in this part of the world. But they couldn't keep the domes up to full size. There's that crystal they need—it won't work forever, and they've about exhausted all the supplies. That's why they had to move all across the ocean. It occurs near volcanic sites. I've been telling them that up above people could make 'em all they wanted, but they won't believe me, and they're no chemists.

"The domes just get weaker and the people sort of give up. Some migrate to other domes. Most of them decide to have smaller families. And the first thing you know, the dome isn't big enough to hold a decent population, and there's so little work everybody practically starves. So far, we've been lucky. But the last crystal hunters almost didn't find the crystals."

Don looked up at the dome and shivered. He could see now why they were worried. With an emergency like that facing them, there was no room left for any serious consideration of such minor things as atom-bombing.

The trouble was that Atlantis had no chemistry to speak of, and had to depend on some natural crystal. And since its science was trial and error instead of organized, it had probably overlooked a great many possible substitutes which theory would have shown to be as good or better. He remembered the huge crystals used in the tuning section; his signal generator, which could be carried in his pocket, would do the same job.

He grinned and stored it away as another weakness. But it wasn't a comfortable grin when Muggins went on. The crystals had a habit of failing suddenly; the ones they had were already old. It was entirely possible that the dome might start collapsing beyond their ability to find substitutes within a few days. Don remembered that in the emergency, his friends were to be "turned over to the sea" first. The sentence suddenly had bitter new meaning.

K'mith was waiting when they arrived at his house. And outside, a huge crowd was waiting with him. It was an angry crowd, and a worried crowd. The dog let out another wail, and faces paled at the sound.

"Bring Shep out," Don said quietly. K'mith nodded, and a minute later Shep came bounding out, jumping up and down and beating his tail into a frenzy. Finally, the dog sat down and stared up at Don happily panting, with his tongue hanging out.

A sigh went up from the crowd, and they began breaking up. "The dog-god smiles," they were muttering, according to Muggins' quick translation. "The prophecy is coming true."

It did look like a smile, Don realized. He picked the

dog up and cradled him over one shoulder, while he turned to face K'mith. "Shall I take him back to the prison with me, my father?" he asked.

K'mith leaned back against the wall of the building and mopped his forehead with his arm. "A few more minutes, and I'd have been in prison," he said. Then he laughed. "I'd like to know how you did that, Don K'Miller to be."

Don smiled slowly. The name was enough. He picked up the dog and went into the house. S'neifa's bed was gone, but his own still stood there. "I think I'll have more freedom if you don't know, sir," he said.

Again K'mith laughed, nodding. "As you wish. But if I find out by myself, you'll return to prison. Will you take my word that you are free for the prevention of a major crisis, and tell me?"

Don showed him the whistle, and nodded. He explained it quickly. The older man shook his head. "Sounds higher than sound," he said slowly. "That was one of the fantasies I didn't believe. When a people have such small secrets, what must their big ones be? I—I wish I could trust your people, my son. With the emergency . . ."

"They could solve it," Don told him. He was sure of it. It would probably take only a small modification of their power handling methods to reduce the need for all the crystal to some small key kernel, with the rest handled electronically in the usual ways. The basic function of parts in the diagram he had seen might be different—but most of the parts had similar working methods among the equipment he knew.

"Then it would have to be soon," K'mith answered. "We have just two of the large spare crystals. And the men whom I sent out a year ago with great supply bubbles have returned to report that they could find no more."

The dome over his head seemed suddenly close and dangerous to Don. He looked up at it, and shivered. The emergency wasn't something for the future now. It was already on them.

He slept fitfully that night, feeling cheap and mean. He'd been using a dirty trick to get out of prison, while K'mith had been faced with the end of his world. And his trick had sent the people who had a real thing to fear into a panic over an imagined one. It seemed like a pretty horrible thing to deny them what comfort they could have while they were living under the dark shadow of death.

He tried again to persuade K'mith that the remedy could be found on the surface world. But when he admitted that he knew of no crystals exactly like the ones they used, the older man signaled him to drop it. Nor would assurances that there were men up there who might know of such crystals change his mind.

"It isn't entirely up to me," he said at last. "I am only the voice of the Council in this. Sometimes I think . . ."

Then he sighed. "But why should I believe you, when the world above is going to its death as quickly as we? How can they help us when they won't help themselves? And today, over our radio, we had word that men on the border of a territory the two nations have divided were engaged in battle."

Don looked at him sickly. War was coming, then. A few such border skirmishes could be passed over, he knew from his history books, but not unless some major change in relations came. And it now looked as if atomic doom were inevitable.

If they could get to the surface with proof of the usefulness of the dome, there still might be time, but it was a matter of hours now, not of days. And there was no transmitter here that he could use, even though Atlantis had a receiver.

He caught himself sharply. The transmitter on the *Triton!* Then he shook his head. Even if Atlantis would let him use it—which they would not—the message would only stay things, until he could prove it was genuine by surfacing. Otherwise, it would be put down to a fake.

K'mith went to the door slowly. "The last spares are now in the dome station," he announced wearily. "If one breaks down . . . well, we can keep the dome up for a few weeks on the smaller crystals in the suits and on the supply bubbles. Or if we cut down to one quarter size, we can keep going until we all starve. Tomorrow . . ."

He stopped, and Don looked up to see his face harden. A cold chill ran through the boy's heart. "Tomorrow?" he asked.

K'mith shook his head. "It's better that you shouldn't know, my son," he said.

But Don knew. Tomorrow, the order for the "mercy of the sea" treatment would go through for his friends.

He had only a few hours left.

CHAPTER 19/

Mad Dog!

DON SQUATTED DOWN on the bunk, digging his fist into his forehead. Shep whined unhappily, but he disregarded the dog. His original idea had been right. He had succeeded, as long as he looked for the other side's weakness to use. But he'd abandoned that to go back to arguing, trying to use the strength of his people's science. It had failed miserably. Now he had to go back to what had worked.

Find the weakness . . . find the weakness . . . find . . .

It was so obvious, when he realized it, that he kicked himself. Their weakness lay in the very trouble that was driving him to this frantic worry. Out there in the dome power station was a weakness that spelled death for all of them. And there were other weaknesses—the superstition that had been encouraged over Shep, for instance. Or the aloofness of the technicians from the people.

The ideal way to gain freedom would be to save Atlantis from its danger, but that was impossible without surface help. Still, if the people thought they were saved, it might work as well. He collected his idea carefully, examined it quickly, and nodded. It wasn't perfect, and would need a lot of changes as he went along. But it was the best he could hope for.

153

"Come on, Shep," he said. The dog was the most doubtful part of his plan. He'd been trained for perfect obedience, but with all the changes in his life, he might get nervous and balk. Like the other weak links in the plan, though, Don had to risk that.

He went out onto the street, noticing the low temper of the people. Most of them couldn't know, but they sensed the danger from those who did. There was nothing they could do. Now they watched the dog in fascination, making their peculiar sign of worship. For a few moments, they seemed to cheer up. But Don knew that even superstition couldn't prop up their lagging hopes forever. It wasn't so much that they believed, as that they didn't dare *not* to believe, in the ancient prophecy of the smiling dog-god.

"The dog-god demands a shrine," he announced to the crowd. "He asks for a place to restore the fortune of Mlayanu. He needs a shrine, and he has chosen one. We go there to save Mlayanu."

Those in the crowd who knew English picked it up. Some translated it with amused contempt, but the crowd missed such subtleties. They began to mutter and collect others.

"Strut!" Don ordered Shep. The dog went up on his hind feet and walked along for a few yards. The crowd gasped again. Don turned to them. "The dog-god finds his godhood rising and goes to make a temple. But there are those who have no faith. They will resist."

He was already sick of the mummery of it, though nobody would be hurt. It had really been K'mith and all the technicians who had encouraged the superstition. Let them see it operate, and maybe they'd be less likely to play on it in the future—if there was a future.

They came to the dome station. "Strut—speak!" he told Shep. The dog obeyed, barking loudly as he danced about.

The technicians came to the front of the station to stare at the scene, but he ignored them. "The dog-god has chosen his shrine," he announced to the crowd which now numbered nearly a thousand. "He must go within to bring strength to the power crystals. He needs only a few minutes. Tell the keepers of the crystals to come out!"

They didn't wait to tell the men inside. They saw Shep start toward the station, barking loudly. Then one man shouted and ran into the forbidden station. Don saw with a shock that it was S'neifa. But the crowd didn't look to see who it was; they had been triggered, and now streamed in behind him.

The technicians weren't having any of the crowd. They shrugged elaborately and came out before they could be removed. One of them turned to Don, glowering. "Be not long," he said in thick English. "If you must be a false priest, be quick. In there we are needed. Ten minutes, not more."

Don nodded quickly. "It's a bargain. Now close the doors."

The crowd streamed out and he went inside. Shep dropped down and followed quietly, unaware of his importance. Don ignored most of the setup and went looking for the main crystals. If he could find something to indicate what they were, he might still get honest help for Atlantis.

He found them, and he could see why the technicians were worried. The big crystals had burned spots that were visible to his eyes, and there were small cracks here and there that had been crudely patched. There was nothing to indicate what type they were.

He traced the diagrams quickly. It did no good. He could guess what the parts were, but the operation of the whole was beyond his knowledge, even in theory. Things were done to a basic electrical signal which could almost certainly be done by transistorized circuits, but he couldn't understand what the results were. It would take a staff of experts to guess. He was sure it could be done. A substitute for the crystals could be found even before the operation was fully understood. But he wasn't well enough trained to do it.

He gave up, and turned to the control section, which he had figured out before. He knew that it depended on a controlling frequency being fed in, to cut the main power off and on, in time with that frequency. The shorter the "off" periods, the less could get through the dome. It was now operating on a frequency of about fifty million a second—which kept the "off" periods down to a fiftieth of a millionth of a second, of course. He found the place where the huge device creating the control signal fed it into the main power section, just as the door burst open.

K'mith led a group of guards, and there was no smile on his face. "This is too much. You have abused our trust for the last time, Don Miller. Play your games elsewhere. You are under arrest." He turned to the guards. "Put him with the others. He's to be the first to be given to the sea in the emergency!"

Don knew better than to argue now. He had known that something like this must happen. He turned to the guards, glancing down at the dog. "Guard the place, Shep!" he ordered softly. The dog dropped back at once and sank to the floor, while the group escorted Don out.

"Hydrophobia!" he cried suddenly. "Don't let him bite you."

"Silence!" K'mith ordered.

It was a long way up the street this time, through the muttering, confused crowd and toward the building that was to be his jail. K'mith walked beside him in stony silence, and the guards seemed eager to use their weapons. Don waited, and still there was no sign from behind. If Shep had failed now . . .

Then the sound of angry barking came to them. Don sighed as it continued. There was a scream of pain, protesting yells, and then mixed shouting of the crowd.

In less than a minute, a group of technicians came raging up the street, followed by a crowd armed with sticks and stones. One of the technicians broke ahead, while the others delayed the mob. His waving arm was gashed and bleeding. Shep had followed orders; nobody was coming into the plant until his master gave him the command to relax his guard.

"Get him out!" The technician screamed to Don. "Get him out! We've got to get in before the dome fails. He's mad!"

Some of the guards dropped back to hold the crowd that was boiling in fury. Their stunguns were effective against the poorly aimed rain of stones, but they looked worried.

Don turned to K'mith. "I told you about hydrophobia," he said, mixing his truth with the smallest amount of outright lying he could use. "It's rare, but it still happens. I guess the high frequency radiation in the station didn't cure him. I don't know whether I can get a mad dog out of there."

"Use your stunguns on him," K'mith ordered.

The technician shook his head violently. "We started to. But the crowd—they would kill us before we hurt him."

K'mith's eyes were suspicious as he turned to Don, but the fear bubbling in the eyes of the technician must have convinced him. "Get him out, then."

"I'll need some equipment from the ship. The antitoxin . . ."

"Then get it." K'mith motioned some of the guards to follow Don, and turned back to the station.

They weren't far from the submarine. Don went up the ramp at full run and dived into the sonar room. The little signal generator lay there, and he pocketed it quickly. He was sweating, but not from exertion. He had no idea of how long the dome could hold without the technicians, or whether it could stand the added strain he was about to put on it.

The guards rushed him through the crowd. At his orders, K'mith reluctantly let them shut the door before he turned to the dog. "All right, Shep," he said. "Take it easy."

He'd need some way of delaying the effect until he got out with Shep. He began looking for a switch to use with some of the twine lying about. A sound behind him swung him around, to face S'neifa crawling out of a pile of boxes. There was some terrific strain going on inside the man, but he came over and began dropping on one knee.

"Thanks," Don told him quickly. S'neifa smiled tightly, still obeying the order not to speak.

Don coupled the signal generator into the circuit, wiring one of the cumbersome switches in ahead of it. With that, the original control equipment would go on working until the switch was thrown. Then the signal generator would take over. Don set it to produce the four hundred cycle "audio" signal he had used for testing. "Wait until I'm outside, S'neifa, and then throw that switch. And I hope I'm right!"

He carried Shep in his arms as he went out, casting a last glance back at the setup. The signal generator and switch would be well hidden. He stepped out—and the trouble began.

Suddenly, from the whole dome around a great roaring note like an organ pipe tuned to G began to sound. The tiny signal of the generator was being amplified and used to turn the great screen off and on four hundred times a second, instead of at the frequency used before. And at that frequency, even liquids should be able to come through during the "off" periods. It was the pressure of the ocean striking the air during those off periods that produced the great humming sound.

He glanced up as a drop of moisture hit him. For the first time in Atlantis, it was raining! Great drops of salt water of the ocean were shooting through the dome and raining down from the top and out from the sides.

The crowd screamed, and began tearing away, milling over each other. The technicians let out their own roars and went tearing into the station. Don jerked his eyes back, but S'neifa had hidden again.

The technicians were going over their controls frantically, changing the setting, and running about like chickens under the attack of a hawk. They were too frantic. The tiny generator with its thin wires hidden away escaped their notice completely. The rain began to puddle on the streets and drizzle on the faces of the sick and frenzied crowd.

Then the technicians broke. One of them rushed up to K'mith, flailing his arms. He shouted out a long string of Atlantean that was almost lost in the cries of the crowd. K'mith turned to Don.

"Are you responsible for this oscillation he's getting?"

Don shrugged. "They *would* have me move the dog-god too soon. Did you see me carry in anything that could do this? Or do you think that an uneducated child could learn your station at once better than all your experts? But if you want, the dog-god and I will try to fix it."

K'mith looked at him for a long moment, then drew him back into the station away from the crowd threatening to overcome the guards. "Fix it! You're educated in your own sciences—I've known that for a long time. But you can't know all of ours, and all the weaknesses of this station. Fix it, before it wrecks the city with fear. And if you can't undo your damages, I shall tear you to bits with my hands before the dome fails!"

Don moved to the big controlling device the Atlanteans had used. He unfastened it completely and shoved it aside—or tried to; even on wheels, it weighed more then he could move. K'mith lent his shoulder unquestioningly, and the bulky machine wheeled reluctantly out of the way. Then Don drew out the tiny-signal generator and cut off the "audio" beat. Outside, the hum disappeared, and a cry came up from the crowd, but he paid no attention to it. He switched to the regular radio frequencies, and turned the indicator until a signal of fifty megacycles would be produced.

Now, with the great dome being turned off and on fifty million times each second, everything was normal again.

"You forced me into this, sir," he told K'mith. "You wouldn't listen to reason. And don't forget now, that to the crowd out there, the dog-god and I have just saved Atlantis from the end you have been expecting. I think I could even persuade them to force you to let me take my friends and go back."

He nodded toward the sounds that were now changing to a wild, joyful singing in which their word for the dog-god was loudest of all. "I never intended to hurt them. I like your people, K'mith, enough to want to save them as much as I want to save my own world. I never tried to do anything that wasn't for their good, too."

K'mith had the signal generator in his hands, turning it over and over. He held it out to the awed technician. "This—or this," he said, pointing first to the tiny device and then to the cumbersome bank of crystals. Then he grimaced, and nodded toward Don. "Go and see what your experiment has done to our crystals."

Don ran back quickly, sudden worry cutting through his triumph. He knew that having the signal operate four hundred times a second meant that it was on for single periods more than a hundred thousand times as long as for a signal of fifty megaherz. He had hoped that it would cancel out, since it was on only a hundred thousandth as many times during a second, too.

But apparently he had been wrong. The great crystals were sicker-looking than before. The burned spots were now glaring wounds, and the cracks had deepened. The technicians were working at them in a frenzied haste.

But it was obvious that they couldn't keep the dome operating much longer.

CHAPTER 20 /

Operation Contact

K'MITH WAS NOT APPARENTLY WORRYING about the crystals when Don went back to him. Seven older men were grouped around him, and two more came dashing up. He held up the signal generator and broke into a slow-paced speech in Atlantean. Their faces had been washed numb by a succession of emotions, but now sudden excitement crept into them.

K'mith handed the tiny generator to Don. "Can it be opened to show the parts?"

Don nodded. He pulled out his pocketknife and found the small screwdriver blade. With it, he removed the screws from the back, and held out the instrument, trying to point out the similar parts in it and in the huge device that was now disconnected. The little transistors, looking like beads of plastic, drew the loudest gasps, though they were closest of all to the crystals the Atlanteans used.

K'mith went back to his speech. Then, with a wave of his hand, he dismissed them. "The Council will meet in an hour," he said in English. "You are with me, I believe?"

The nine men who must be Councilors nodded, though some did it with reluctance. K'mith waited for them to leave, and then smiled grimly to himself. He motioned to the head technician, who had been standing impatiently.

"How long will the crystals last?"

"Perhaps ten minutes—no more," the man said. "Shall I put in the good crystals now?"

K'mith's smile deepened, and he nodded. At once, a crew of the men began digging into the boxes lying around, at the orders of the head technician. Their amazement was as genuine as that of Don as they began to remove new crystals in perfect condition.

"You were playing your game, Don K'Miller," K'mith said. "And I was playing my own desperate one. For twenty years, I have tried to approach the surface world, as my brother did before me. But the Council has always vetoed me by a slim majority. When the emergency began to creep up on us, I built up a false crisis ahead of time, in order to scare them into action in time—just as you created one for your purposes. Now that they have seen how a handful of material from the surface can do more than all their massive equipment and ancient knowledge permits—and now that they have felt the horror of an emergency upon them—yes, I think they are convinced."

He held out his hand. "We come from different worlds, my son who is now K'Miller—but in our own ways, we seem to think much the same. And when men think alike, how can they be of *different* worlds? They are only of separated worlds."

"But—" Don took his foster father's hand slowly, still trying to catch his mental breath. "But then—there was no emergency."

"There would have been in less than another year. Those ten good crystals have been hoarded for a long time. The expedition that could find no more crystals was an honest one. I've fooled you in some ways; I've even had my—my daughter secretly educated, to find whether the surface world could start education at such an early age. I've pretended that I believed none of what I heard and read in the books, in order to keep from being removed from the Council. But the emergency was real—so real and so close that I had to do many things to meet it."

Don felt better, in a way. He'd been guilty of pretending a few things himself, because he had to. But it would have hurt to think that his efforts had been all wasted on a danger which had never existed.

"And what about my people and the submarine?" he asked.

K'mith smiled. "I've already sent guards to release your friends, and the submarine is being prepared for the trip back. We will even install a permanent bubble-of-force generator and control on it. With heavy glass tips to the outlets and inlets of your jets to keep the bubble from touching there, we can arrange it so you will find the bubble no hindrance to navigation, even. You'll also find that our antenna has been connected to your transmitter, if you want to contact the surface. And K'Miller, my son—work as hard now to save us as you have in the past. The dome-control secret is yours. Get us the help of your science!"

"You'll get it," Don promised, and he was sure of it. With the margin of the new crystals, there would be time enough for the best brains of earth to find the answers. "But there's one thing more."

"And that?"

"S'neifa." Don moved back toward the packing boxes from which the last of the crystals was being removed, and motioned for his friend. "Come on out."

"You!" K'mith said bitterly as the young man stood up awkwardly, but with a strange pride to his humbleness. Then, slowly, the older man's face melted. "Yes," he said at last. "Yes, there is my son, S'neifa. Let us wipe out all the bitterness of this affair."

He held out his arms, and S'neifa jumped forward with a low cry, his face beaming as he cast a single glance at Don. Then his legs faltered. His voice was an effort as he cleared his throat. "I can't ask forgiveness, my Father. I did what I had to do. I'd do it again."

"You stubborn fool!" K'mith said hoarsely. "Do you think I'd take you back any other way? Come here!"

Don moved off, trying to adjust to the reaction inside himself and to realize that it was all over now, except for the message back to the surface. That would be difficult, until he could wear away suspicions of the people up there and convince them. But there could be no war now, with the secret of the dome given to all the world. Other separated worlds would have a chance to learn that they were not different, after all, and to relax and build for the future in safety.

He moved toward the submarine with Shep trotting along behind him. From the jail building, he saw the rest of his people coming out and stopped to wave at them, before going on. But there was time to get together, after his message. They'd soon all be together, going home.

In that, he was wrong. As he stood outside the *Triton* four days later, he was patting Shep good-by. He looked up at K'mith's daughter, as he handed over the dog's leash "For keeping a secret," he said. "And because Shep likes you."

She dropped into the automatic deep curtsy of Mlayanu girls, but her eyes were dancing with pleasure. "You'll be back," she said. "I'll keep him for you, Don!"

Then she blushed and hurried off, her training conflicting with her knowledge that there was nothing wrong to him in what she had said. He grinned after her, knowing she was right. He'd be back. But for the time, Shep was needed here, until the people could feel fresh hope without the need of superstition.

Don moved up the ramp to watch the others come on board. Drake and his uncle were still admiring the changes the Atlanteans had made in the jets to enable the *Triton* to work while the bubble of force protected her. He heard Simpson's voice. ". . . the last of her type, as well as the first. They'll build them light now, since they have the force field."

Don hadn't thought of that. He ran his hand affectionately over the ship. But progress had to go on, and he knew the two men would soon be busy with new designs.

The little cook came up, grinning. "Coffee in the wardroom, sir," he said, and ducked back down again.

The crewmen were already aboard, still stowing the last of the material they were taking up from Atlantis. Haller came up for a last look, just as Kayne began mounting the ramp. The navigator hesitated nervously, and then came on.

"Welcome aboard, Mr. Kayne," Haller said quietly.

The navigator stumbled, and tears came into his eyes. "I—I—" he said. Then he ducked down into the ship.

Haller shrugged. "The end of the bitterness. I'll have to have him released. He isn't fit for service. But there are ways of doing it painlessly. Come on, Don."

They went down into the wardroom for the coffee. K'mith was there ahead of them, tasting the beverage doubtfully as S'neifa urged it on him. Walrich and Cavanaugh were finishing theirs, and they went out to their posts as Haller left. In a corner, Upjohn was already busy on a typewriter, getting the story ready that was to make history. He waved a lazy arm, and went back to his machine, while S'neifa came over to stare at it again in fascination.

The young Atlantean would be the first from the sea world to attend the universities of the surface, once the final red tape was straightened out.

Then the sound of the hatches being closed reached Don's ears, and he headed back toward the sonar room. Even with the bubble on, the instruments would work now, since their pickups had also been mounted on glass, and removed from the hull enough to make sure they were beyond the bubble of force.

They would head nearly straight up, cruising slowly in a spiral to give a full test to the *Triton's* new devices. At the surface, the ships that were to escort them back to the mainland were already waiting—ships of both

nations, already celebrating the end of the short but ter-
rifying threat of war.

"Sharp, now," Haller said to Don. "I want to surface
exactly in the center of our escort, Mr. Miller. We can't
be sloppy about things now."

"Sharp it is, sir," Don answered.

Dexter came into the sonar room then, with K'mith
and Kenney waiting behind him. "Too late to send another message to the President?" the man asked. He'd
been busy with communications since the first message
had gone up, and had been largely instrumental in getting the surface convinced of the truth of Don's first
broadcast.

"Afraid so, sir," Don told him.

Dexter shrugged goodnaturedly. "All right. No matter. I merely wanted to report that his suggestion had
been accepted by President K'mith and Senator Kenney.
But it can wait."

Don glanced up at Kenney, wondering at the smile
on the man's face as he faced K'mith. He cocked an ear
and listened.

"Yes, sir," he heard Kenney saying. "I knew it was
right the minute you agreed. Be glad to retire from the
Senate, now that Dexter here tells me he's sure the
President will go along with your idea of having me for
ambassador. You won't regret it. No, sir. I may be an
old man, but I'm not finished yet."

K'mith winked at Don as they went back toward the
wardroom. An end to bitterness, he had said. Don wondered if that wasn't carrying things a bit too far. But he
had an idea K'mith usually knew what he was doing.

Haller issued a final order, and the *Triton* began to
slip smoothly from the pool, while one of the pickups
showed the cheering crowd fading behind them. Then
there was a lurch as they were through the dome and
moving upward.

Don swung back to the sonar screen, slipping into the
work for which he'd prepared himself. Dexter had told
him he'd get a medal; it was flattering enough, but he'd

had enough of playing the half-baked hero to last for the rest of his life.

He settled down to his work as the *Triton* headed up for the calm seas and bright skies awaiting on the surface.